SECRETS of the X-POINT

ESCAPED

SECRETS of the X-POINT

ESCAPED

GARY UREY

ALBERT WHITMAN & COMPANY
CHICAGO, ILLINOIS

Also by Gary Urey
Secrets of the X-Point: *Pursued*

Names: Urey, Gary, author. | Brundage, Scott, illustrator.
Title: Escaped / Gary Urey; pictures by Scott Brundage.
Description: Chicago, Illinois: Albert Whitman & Company, 2017. |
Series: Secrets of the X-Point; 2 | Summary: "After Daisha and Axel destroy the
permanent X-point, they must expose a new one in order to stabilize Earth's
magnetic field, all while evading a doomsday cult"—Provided by publisher.
Identifiers: LCCN 2017039783 | ISBN 9780807566893 (paperback)
Subjects: | CYAC: Science fiction. | Adventure and adventurers—Fiction. |
BISAC: JUVENILE FICTION / Action & Adventure / Survival Stories. |
JUVENILE FICTION / Science & Technology. | JUVENILE FICTION /
Social Issues / Friendship.
Classification: LCC PZ7.U67 Esc 2017 | DDC [Fic]—dc23
LC record available at https://lccn.loc.gov/2017039783

Text copyright © 2018 by Gary Urey
Cover art copyright © 2018 by Scott Brundage
First published in the United States of America in 2018 by Albert Whitman & Company
All rights reserved. No part of this book may be reproduced or transmitted in any
form or by any means, electronic or mechanical, including photocopying,
recording, or by any information storage and retrieval system,
without permission in writing from the publisher.

Printed in the United States of America
10 9 8 7 6 5 4 3 2 1 LB 22 21 20 19 18

Design by Jordan Kost

For more information about Albert Whitman & Company,
visit our website at www.albertwhitman.com.

For Jill Corcoran

Chapter One
AXEL

Hot, acrid smoke seared Axel Jack's lungs as Jag carried him piggyback-style along a narrow footpath. Exploded chunks of satellite dishes, x-ray lasers, and dozens of other pieces of high-tech equipment rained down around them. A stab of intense pain surged through Axel's leg. He looked down and saw blood soaking his pants, right where Doctor Lennon Hatch had plunged a knife at the Konanavlah Sun Temple.

The maniacal billionaire and his Pursuers had chased Axel and his best friend, Daisha Tandala, around the globe for six months, trying to get their GeoPorts. The temple was supposed to be the new site of the Doctor's Geographical Transportation hub. But fortunately for the world, things had not gone according to plan.

"I'm going to need stitches," Axel groaned.

"You'll have medical attention soon," Jag said, hoisting Axel higher on his back.

Jag's large, quiet presence had given Axel the creeps when they had first met at the Sun Temple. Now, he felt indebted to the man. Without him and Megan, the Stanford research assistant who had helped his father and Daisha's mother make Geographical Transportation possible, he'd probably be lying dead among the ruins right now.

"Where are we going?" Megan asked, huffing for breath.

"Bhimbetka rock shelters, just a few kilometers. That's where the others from the Sun Temple have gone. We'll be safe there."

The Konanavlah Sun Temple faded into the distance as Jag led them over a small stream and into a dense jungle. Screeching alarm calls from a troop of langur monkeys rang from treetops. Insects buzzed around Axel's head; exotic birds flittered from branch to branch.

Jag stopped in his tracks, and Axel felt all of the muscles in his friend's back tighten. He cautiously peered over Jag's shoulder and nearly passed out from what he saw. A five-hundred-pound Bengal tiger lay crouched behind a fallen tree just ten yards ahead. The animal stared at them, ears pinned back, tail swishing in the breeze.

"Get behind me," Jag ordered.

"It probably smells my blood," Axel said, heart pounding.

"Should we run?" Megan whispered.

Jag slowly edged them back. "That would be a death sentence," he said. "Just like a house cat, tigers enjoy the thrill of the chase. Our only chance is to not act like its natural prey."

Fortunately, they didn't have to test the tiger's patience for very long. Another piece of the Doctor's equipment blasted in the distance. The loud boom and ensuing black smoke made the animal leap five feet into the air and take off into the jungle.

"We're safe," Jag said, leading them back up the path. "That cat is too frightened to stalk us now."

Axel wasn't so sure. He kept looking over his shoulder every few seconds to make sure the tiger wasn't following them. It had been hard enough to make it away from the exploding Sun Temple alive. The last thing they needed was another—deadlier—Pursuer.

The jungle soon opened up into a vibrant green field dotted with palm trees. A well-traveled dirt road wound its way around a large body of water leading toward a village.

Several noisy motorcycles whizzed past them, followed by a rusty truck stuffed with a load of green bananas. People and houses came into view. A young girl led a leashed cow to a water trough. Two men took turns pounding some kind of grain in a large mortar. Among the bustle of the village, it didn't seem anyone knew of the chaos that had just taken place a few short kilometers away. If they had, they'd already moved on.

The trio turned a corner and came to an open-air market. Jasmine and lavender incense wafted in the air. The spicy smells of cinnamon, saffron, coriander, curry, and freshly baked naan filled Axel's nostrils. His stomach grumbled with hunger. He loved eating Indian food at the Amber Elephant back in Palo Alto, but this was the real thing.

People stared at them as they made their way through the crowd.

"I guess it's not every day the locals see a tall Indian man carrying a wounded white boy on his back," Axel said.

"Everything smells so good," Megan said. "I'm so—"

"We must get to Bhimbetka first," Jag said, reading her mind. "Then we will eat."

Axel gasped.

Jag and Megan looked up and saw what had alarmed him.

Pursuers.

There were two of them, wearing their black jackets and white shirts, skulking around the market.

"After all that's happened, the Doctor's still looking for us," Megan whispered, her voice slightly trembling.

"Well, if someone just thwarted my attempt at world domination, I would be searching for them too," Axel whispered, mustering a slight grin.

One of the men whipped out an eight-by-ten photo and showed it to a young girl standing among the baskets of okra, ginger, and red peppers.

"Follow me," Jag said, grabbing Megan's arm.

They hurried through the market and down a dark alley. A skinny cow rested in a bed of mud. A rat darted from behind a barrel and disappeared under a stack of wooden pallets. They were almost at the end of the alley when a middle-aged man with a suspicious look on his face stepped out of the shadows and blocked their way.

"Why are you carrying the boy?" the man asked in choppy English. "Is he a cripple?"

"Let us pass," Jag said.

The man stepped closer and stared at Axel's face. "You're the one in the picture—the one the two Europeans are showing around the market. They offered a reward for you!"

Before the man could alert anyone, Jag charged into him. The man tumbled roughly to the ground. A set of keys fell from his hand. Megan scooped them up, and they ran from the alley. An old, rust-caked Honda motorcycle sat parked on the street. Jag slipped Axel off his back, hopped onto the motorcycle, and jammed the keys into the ignition. The engine roared to life.

"We need to go!" Jag hollered. "Now!"

Megan helped Axel onto the back of the seat, and she climbed on too. He wrapped his arms around Jag's waist and held on tight. His jeans were completely blood soaked and sticky. With a shift of the gears, the motorcycle lurched forward, and they tore away from the village.

Countryside, farm fields, and rolling hills filled Axel's vision. Simple mud huts teetered on the side of a bumpy road. The thump of the motorcycle riding over potholes made the wound in Axel's leg pulse with pain. His head started spinning, bright spots danced in front of his eyeballs, and all the strength ran out of his arms. He let go of Jag and slumped to one side.

Megan grabbed Axel's shoulders to keep him from falling off the speeding motorcycle.

"He's losing lots of blood!" she yelled over the sound of the motorcycle.

Jag pulled to the side of the road. He took off his shirt and handed it to Megan. She tore it into strips, making a temporary tourniquet, and tied it several inches above Axel's wound.

A few moments later, Axel regained consciousness, feeling nauseous but slightly better. They continued riding for almost an hour until the motorcycle choked to a stop.

"What's the matter?" Megan asked.

"Out of petrol," Jag said.

"What's petrol?" Axel wondered aloud.

Jag wheeled to the side of the road. "It's another name for gasoline," he said. "We must walk the rest of the way."

Jag helped Axel onto his back, and they hiked deep into the jungle. They came upon a sign that said *Ratapani Tiger Reserve* in both Hindi and English.

"Please, no more tigers," Axel groaned.

A chuckle escaped from Jag's lips. "Don't worry," he said. "The Bhimbetka rock shelters are within the reserve's boundaries."

After hiking through more jungle, five massive sandstone outcrops surrounded by a wire fence came into view. Tourists crowded around a large information board.

"We're here," Jag said, scooting Axel off his back and leaning against a tree to catch his breath.

"Is this some kind of tourist attraction?" Axel asked. His head had started spinning again, making his vision blurry and stomach queasy.

"It's a lot more than just that," Megan said, pointing toward a large inscribed brass plaque. "This is a designated UNESCO World Heritage Site."

"Come," Jag said, lifting Axel onto his back. "Larraj will be waiting for us."

They followed behind a large tour group that stopped every few meters to gaze in awe at the prehistoric paintings. There were depictions that looked to be from the Stone Age of people hunting with bows and arrows. There were drawings of elephants, horses, tigers, and deer. When everyone stopped to look at a painted figure of a god believed to be Nataraja, Jag broke away from the group and Axel followed with Megan's help. Jag led them through an extremely narrow cavern. The space was so tight, that in some points, Jag had to turn sideways to pass through. The cavern finally opened up to a pile of impenetrable boulders.

"It's a dead end," Megan said.

"Why'd you take us here?" Axel wondered aloud.

Jag didn't answer. He gripped a very large round stone and heaved it aside.

Axel looked closer. "It's a hole."

"More than a hole," Jag said. "Larraj should be waiting for us below."

"Are you telling us we have to crawl into this snake pit?" Megan asked with a grimace.

"Yes," Jag answered. "This is the entrance to another cave, one not known to tourists or the local population. Its secret location was revealed to Larraj on one of the palm leaves. We have to go single file. You two first."

Megan reluctantly crawled into the opening, and Axel limped forward. Waves of claustrophobia surged through his veins. Searing pain burned through his wounded leg.

"I really don't want to do this," he protested.

"Go," Jag commanded. "We'll get help for your leg."

Axel took a deep breath and lowered into the hole.

Chapter Two

DAISHA

Daisha and Boris the dog left the Stanford campus and jogged up Embarcadero Road. Streetlights burned bright, but because it was past midnight, nearly all of the houses were dark. The one she and her mother used to live in was only a couple blocks away on Byron Street. It was the little white bungalow with the powder-blue shutters in need of a paint job. A cascade of childhood memories flooded her mind. Playing hide-and-seek in the backyard, the traveling petting zoo party for her seventh birthday, and the cheap plastic swimming pool, always filled with freezing cold hose water.

The rumble of a car engine ripped her back to the present. Boris let out a low growl. Daisha grabbed the dog by the scruff of the neck and gently pulled him behind a tree. She watched a blue pickup truck slowly cruise past them and pull into a driveway. When the driver parked the truck and disappeared into a house, Daisha and Boris continued down the sidewalk.

"Axel, how in the world am I supposed to find you again?" she wondered aloud.

Daisha wasn't even sure if he was dead or alive. The last image she had of him was with the Doctor's hand clamped around his neck.

"You're alive," she muttered, a lump forming in her throat. "I know it."

Her eyes grew misty. Just thinking about him made her want to cry. She fought the urge, reached into her pocket, and felt something hard and round.

"Axel's GeoPort!" Daisha exclaimed. She remembered dropping hers and scooping his off the ground just as the Sun Temple was about to implode. The Warp had sucked her into the stratosphere so hard and fast she forgot all about the GeoPort.

She cradled the unit in her palms, fingers trembling, thumbs frantically pressing buttons. There was nothing. The thing was dead. Tears streamed down her face. Without the X-Point, the biggest technological advancement of mankind was now as useless as a floppy disk. She and Axel had fulfilled their parents' dying wish by keeping Geographical Transportation out of the Doctor's grubby hands, but now finding Axel would be next to impossible.

Unless.

Maybe he was able to use his GeoPort one last time before everything shut down, she thought. If so, he'd go to one place—the Hoover Park Dog Run.

Feelings of hope and fear tingled in her chest. The dog area wasn't only their prearranged meeting place. It was also the location where her mother and Axel's dad had been killed and where the Doctor's henchman Loosha had almost captured her.

Daisha wiped away tears and stroked Boris's head. She did not want to go back there ever again, but she had no choice.

"Let's go, boy," she said, taking a deep breath. "If Axel's here, that's where we'll find him."

One question twirled in her mind as they turned up Cowper Street toward the park: Why am I still alive?

Megan had set Axel's GeoPort for the heart of the sun. The purpose had been to destroy the X-Point—the place where the Earth's magnetic field connected to the sun's and the key to the GeoPort's power—in order to make the Doctor's plan for Geographical Transportation impossible. And it seemed to have worked. After all, the GeoPort was dead. But if the plan had worked, how was she back in Palo Alto, unharmed and not one jot worse for the wear?

Daisha shook the thoughts from her head. No matter how she was still alive, she needed to keep her wits about her. Even though she and Axel had thwarted the Doctor's plan, he could still have people searching for them.

Hoover Park was silent and empty. Tall trees cast long shadows over the green lawns from the streetlights. A swing's chain creaked in the wind. The pungent smell from a skunk wafted in the air, making Boris's tail wag and setting his nose to the ground.

"Don't get any ideas," Daisha warned the dog. "I don't have tomato juice or a bathtub to clean you up."

They walked quietly across the softball field to the playground. Daisha's heart pounded with every step. She stopped at a climbing web and leaned against the slide. The dog area was just beyond the basketball court and through a stand of trees.

Horrifying memories of the place bubbled to the surface, and she quickly stamped them down. She ran a nervous hand across her shorn scalp, all of her senses on high alert. Every ounce of her being wanted to turn around and run away as fast as she could. But the faint hope of a reunion with Axel was too strong. She nudged

Boris with her foot and stepped closer to the trees. They walked down a small footpath, opened the gate, and stepped inside the Dog Run. Like the rest of the park, the fenced-off area was empty.

Feelings of relief and sadness swept over her. She was happy that no Pursuers seemed to be hiding in the shadows ready to pounce—maybe the Doctor and his goons were finally off her back, after all. But that was a small comfort compared to the sadness of not seeing Axel there waiting.

The sound of Boris moving around snapped her out of her trance. The dog was looking the other way with his ears perked up. He started to growl and gave a series of woofs.

"What's wrong?" Daisha whispered. "You better not mess with that skunk."

Satisfied there was no threat, Boris went back to sniffing and lifting a leg to mark his territory.

Where should I go now? Daisha thought. And how do I find Axel?

Thoughts of turning herself into the Palo Alto Police Department briefly passed through her mind, but she quickly dismissed them. She knew the police would never believe her story about the X-Point, Warping to the sun, the Doctor, or the murder of her mother and Axel's father. Besides, with all the news coverage of her and Axel's disappearances, if she resurfaced now, she'd be plastered across every news website and TV station across the country. That was the last thing she needed.

Her faith in adults had disappeared many months ago. The only person in the world she could truly trust was Axel, and he was nowhere to be found.

A round of loud barks from Boris again shattered the quiet. The dog had switched from aimless sniffing to full protection mode in the snap of a finger. His ears were pinned back, and his lips curled into a snarl, revealing razor-sharp teeth.

"Who's there?" Daisha called.

There was no response.

Crunching sounds came from the other side of the Dog Run. Boris growled louder and snapped his jaws.

"Stay back!" Daisha cried, still unable to see who or what was approaching. "I'll sic my dog on you! He'll bite!"

"*Dziewczyna*," a deep voice grumbled in the darkness.

Dziewczyna.

The foreign yet strangely familiar word flooded into her ears. Daisha reached deep into her mind, desperately trying to remember where she had heard it before.

"Loosha," she hushed to herself, finally realizing the source. He was one of the Doctor's Pursuers. The last place she had seen him was right in this very spot, when Boris ripped a chunk of flesh out of his arm and Axel beat him with a fallen tree branch.

The tall, muscular man emerged from behind a tree, making Daisha's insides shatter like a sheet of ice. The bull tattoo on the side of his neck gleamed in the moonlight. His thick accent was unmistakable.

"Remember me?" Loosha said, aiming a pistol at her.

Boris instinctively leaped at him. Loosha reeled back on his heels and fired at the dog. With a blast of smoke, Boris let out a yelp and fell to the dirt. Daisha turned to run and heard another shot. Sharp, slicing pain tore through her right hip. She stumbled to the ground and reached for the injury. She expected to feel a wound left by a bullet, but instead discovered a small, feathered dart penetrating her skin.

"Wha...wha...what do you want?" Daisha panted.

Loosha leaned over her. "I knew you'd come back here," he said.

Daisha looked up at him. Her eyelids fluttered, head bobbing like it was too heavy for her neck, and she passed out cold.

Chapter Three

AXEL

After wiggling for a few yards, Axel dropped into a large, subterranean chamber lit with torches. He took one step and crumpled to the ground.

"Owww!" he cried out as excruciating pain sliced through his wounded leg.

Megan rushed to his side. "Help!" she hollered, her panicked voice echoing off the cave walls. "We have a wounded kid here!"

People emerged from the shadows. Axel looked up and saw two dancers from the Sun Temple, a man and a girl who looked to be about his age.

"Treat his wound immediately," Jag ordered.

The two dancers lifted Axel off the floor and carried him down a long, dark passageway. Ancient murals and carvings covered the rock walls: a four-armed man, swans, snakes, elephants, exotic birds, and several god-like figures seated in a lotus position.

They passed through a beaded curtain and into another room. The place glowed orange from several lit candles. Smoke from jasmine-scented incense wafted in the air. Elegant tapestries of Hindu gods decorated the walls.

"Where am I?" Axel asked as the two dancers laid him down on a cot filled with pillows.

"One of the sleeping chambers," the girl said with a thick Indian accent.

"I'll get the medical supplies," the man said as he exited the room.

The girl produced a knife and sliced away Axel's pant leg.

"What are you doing?" Axel said in protest.

"I'm exposing the wound so it can be cleaned. You don't want these soiled pants anyway."

When the girl removed the pant leg, Axel saw his wound for the first time—a deep gash three inches long. Dried blood and exposed flesh spilled around the cut. The look of it made Axel even more light-headed than he already was.

The girl dabbed a white cloth in a pail of water and started wiping away the blood.

"Ouch," Axel moaned. "I'm going to need a dozen stitches."

"A lot more than that, I'm afraid," the girl said, trying to be as gentle as possible. "My name's Charu. You're Axel, right? Larraj told me a lot about you."

A shiver went up Axel's spine as he remembered the mystical Larraj reading Daisha's and his palm leaves back at the Sun Temple. Even though they had never met the Nadi reader in their lives, he had known their names, ages, places of birth, and other personal information. He even knew about the Doctor, that their parents were scientists, *and* how they had lost their lives.

The boy with hair like a muddy river must die yet still live.

The prophecy Larraj had revealed back at the Konanavlah Sun Temple came into Axel's mind. So did Daisha. Axel's heart clenched and tears formed at the corners of his eyes. Larraj's palm leaf prophecy had gotten it completely correct. Without Daisha, Axel felt dead inside. Yet, he was still alive.

"Larraj explained to me in intimate detail my palm leaf prophecy," Axel said after a moment. "Who knew I was so popular in this part of the world?"

Charu chuckled. It made Axel feel good to hear laughter again. He studied her face. She was young, probably a teenager not much older than him, with large dark eyes and black hair. Glistening in the center of her forehead was a red dot. Axel knew this was called a *bindi*, but he had no idea what it meant.

Charu caught his eye. "Let me guess: You want to know what my bindi represents?"

"Uh...I didn't mean any disrespect," said Axel, fidgeting.

Charu smiled. "Don't worry. I get it all the time from tourists who visit the temple."

Axel grimaced in pain as she cleaned closer to the wound.

"Perhaps we'll have time later," Charu said. "There is a lot to tell, and I need to concentrate."

The other dancer came back into the room, carrying a canvas bag with the words *Suture Kit* written on the outside. The man looked to be in his twenties. He was bare-chested with long gold beads draped around his neck. His loose, silky pants were the iridescent blue and green colors of a peacock. His costume perfectly matched Charu's elegant purple and gold sari.

"Is he ready?" the man asked.

Charu shook her head. "Antiseptic," she said.

The man rummaged through the bag, pulled out a brown bottle, and handed it to her.

"This is going to sting," Charu said. "Are you ready?"

Axel nodded and closed his eyes. When the antiseptic flowed over the wound, he let out an anguished cry. Charu dabbed at the wound and poured on more cleaner, each dose more painful than the last. When she had sanitized the area, the man knelt beside Axel.

"My name is Kundan," he said. "Don't worry. I've stitched up many wounds. The scar will be barely visible after healing."

Kundan put on a pair of rubber gloves and rubbed a white cream around the wound. Instantly, the area grew numb.

"Hand me the scissors and tissue forceps," Kundan ordered Charu.

Charu rolled her eyes. "Yes, Your Highness," she said sarcastically as she retrieved the items from the canvas bag.

Kundan loaded thread into a curved needle and went to work closing the wound.

"That should do it," Kundan said when he had finished. He wiped away the excess antiseptic and covered the wound with a large bandage.

"How do you feel?" Charu asked.

Axel shrugged. "Like I just got about twenty-five stitches."

"I'll be back later," Kundan said. "Try not to move around too much. And don't worry, the men who were chasing you will never find you down here."

Kundan pulled off the rubber gloves, tossed them in a trash pail, and left the room.

The room grew brighter. Axel craned his neck and saw that Charu had lit a torch hanging from the wall.

"Why didn't you light that before Kundan started stitching me up?" Axel asked. "He could have seen better."

"His Highness saw just fine," Charu said. She poured a glass of cold water from a pitcher and handed it to Axel. "Drink this. You need to keep hydrated."

Axel sat up, tilted the glass to his lips, and chugged the water down in three giant gulps.

"You don't like Kundan very much, do you?" Axel asked.

Charu made the international symbol for *Loser* by raising a hand to her forehead and extending her index finger and thumb. Then she became more serious.

"He's all right," she said. "He *wanted* to be a temple dancer. I mostly do it because my parents expect me to."

"I know what that's like," said Axel. "Well—I guess my parents didn't know any of this would happen, but I've been on the run for months because of what my dad and Daisha's mom discovered."

"Perhaps this can be a new start." Charu smiled. She poured Axel another glass of water and picked his bloody pants off the floor. As she was walking to the trash pail, something round and hard fell from the pocket. The item skittered across the floor and landed just out of Axel's reach.

"It's my GeoPort," Axel said.

The memories attached to the unit made his chest swell with both anger and sadness. With everything that happened back at the temple, running through the jungle on Jag's back, and now these caves, he had forgotten all about it. Then he realized it was actually Daisha's. She had dropped hers right before hurtling into the sky. As Jag and Megan hauled him to safety, he had scooped the GeoPort up and shoved it into his pocket.

As he thought back to the events that brought him to the caves, a tear leaked down his cheek. He wiped it away and tried reaching for the GeoPort.

It couldn't be a new start for Axel like it was for Charu. Not yet. He needed to find out what happened to Daisha.

"Hand me the GeoPort, please. I can't reach it."

Charu picked up the GeoPort and handed it to him. "What is it? A new type of phone?"

"It's a...well, it's...I'll explain another time," Axel said, not even knowing where to begin.

He tapped at the buttons, trying to turn it on. The thing was dead. Without an X-Point, there was no more Geographical Transportation. Without Geographical Transportation, there was no immediate way back to Palo Alto. Could Daisha possibly be alive? If so, was she waiting for him back at the Hoover Park Dog Run?

The Doctor and his Pursuers flashed in Axel's mind, making his heart swell with fury. "This thing's a curse!" he cried, hurling the GeoPort across the room. "I never want to see it again!"

Chapter Four
DAISHA

A series of loud rumbles ripped Daisha from her sleep. She opened her eyes, sat up, and saw the walls shaking. Beside her, a pitcher of water rattled off a nightstand and crashed to the floor. Dust rained down on her from above. She looked up at the ceiling and saw a small fissure working its way across the sheetrock.

Her heart raced, and sweat poured down her cheeks.

"What's happening?" she called out.

Then everything grew quiet, as if someone had flipped a switch to *off*.

Daisha rubbed her eyes.

"Was I just in an earthquake?" she mumbled groggily.

Seismic activity wasn't that uncommon where she was from in California. Usually, the quakes were minor. There were a lot of 2.9s—maybe a 4.0 every now and again—barely enough to feel anything at all. But this one was much bigger, at least a 6.0 or higher.

"Where the heck am I?" she wondered, glancing around at the strange surroundings.

She was lying on a soft bed, wrapped in a fluffy comforter, inside an elegant-looking bedroom. Fancy artwork, now crooked from the tremor, hung from the walls. Rays of bright sunshine streamed in through the large windows. There was a door leading to a stone patio, and just beyond that was a swimming pool and well-manicured lawn. A pile of black-and-white fur lay crumpled next to a dresser.

"Boris!" Daisha exclaimed.

She jumped out of bed and stumbled to him. For a panic-stricken second, Daisha thought the dog was dead, but then she saw the gentle lifting and falling of his chest. Slowly, the events of the previous night re-played in her mind. She had blasted through the Warp, heading directly to the heart of the sun. Then, just as she had been about to plunge headfirst into a fiery solar death, she'd landed at Centennial fountain, and Boris had been waiting for her. They'd made their way to Hoover Park, hoping Axel would be there.

A sharp, needling pain shot across her right hip. She reached down and felt a bandage, one that she hadn't placed there.

"Loosha," she said out loud. "The scumbag shot Boris and I with some kind of tranquilizer dart."

She walked groggily across the room and gave the door a tug. Someone had locked it from the *outside*. She tried the patio doors. Same thing. With a grunt, she picked up a heavy marble sculpture of a lion beside the patio door and hurled it at the window, trying to escape. It didn't work. The sculpture bounced off the window like the glass was made of rubber. She had to step out of the way of the sculpture flying back at her.

Footsteps pounded outside her door.

The bedroom door flew open. Loosha and an older woman wearing pink nursing scrubs stepped inside. Daisha didn't recognize the woman, but Loosha was exactly as she remembered him from Hoover Park, tall and muscular, with buzzed blond hair and a bull tattoo on the side of his neck. A holstered pistol dangled from his side.

Anger boiled inside Daisha's heart. She charged at him, fists flailing, trying to get out the door. Loosha grabbed her by the shoulders and flung her hard to the floor. The man was too big for her to get past. And this time Boris wasn't in any state to help her.

"Let me go!" she cried.

"Try that again, *dziewczyna*," Loosha said in his

thick accent, "and you and I will have big problems."

"Please, sir," the nurse said, her voice filled with concern. "The girl's had a rough—"

Loosha shot the nurse an icy glare, instantly quieting her. "You've bandaged her hip fine," he said through gritted teeth. "I will take over from here."

The nurse gave a resigned nod and stepped out of the room.

"That was some quake," Loosha said when the nurse had left. "Lucky all the windows are made from earthquake-resistant glass. Otherwise, the Doctor's house crew would have a mess to clean up."

"What do you want with me?" Daisha asked, her muscles tense in case she had to defend herself against him.

"I think it's the other way around," Loosha said, slowly moving toward her. "What do *you* want from *me*?"

"I don't want anything from you! Where am I?"

"You're on the Doctor's property in one of his guest cottages. I live here too."

An audible groan escaped from Daisha's lips. Her last memory of the Doctor was when he had plunged his knife into Axel's leg.

"Is Axel here?" she asked, hoping the Pursuer would say yes.

Loosha shook his head. "As far as I know, he's still in India. The Doctor is too, and he'll be there for quite a while. He and his little cockroach sidekick, Pinchole, have a lot of explaining to do for blowing up that temple."

"Is Axel de—" Daisha started to say, but couldn't bear to say the words.

"Dead? Is that what you want to know?"

Daisha nodded.

Loosha shrugged. "I don't know or care. The Doctor already paid me for capturing him. I thought you'd put more *pieniądze* in my pocket, but I was wrong."

"What are you talking about?"

"My friends back at the Doctor's headquarters just told me he doesn't want you anymore. It was a big waste of my time staking out that park and waiting for you."

"Then let me go."

"Not quite yet. I may still get *something* for you."

Loosha brushed by her and knelt down beside Boris. With a scowl, he lifted Boris's head and examined the dog's teeth.

"I paid two thousand dollars for this Karelian." He held up his heavily bandaged right hand. "And this is the type of loyalty I get in return. He was supposed to protect *me*, not *you*."

"Maybe if you hadn't beat and kicked him, he'd like you better," Daisha said, remembering her captor hurting the dog right before the attack at Hoover Park.

"*Dziewcz—*" Loosha started to say, but Daisha interrupted him.

"My name's Daisha. D.A.I.S.H.A. Not *dziewczyna*."

Loosha chuckled. "For such a young *dziewczyna—*"

A loud chirping sound bounced off the walls.

"Where's that noise coming from?" Loosha asked.

Daisha's heart soared. She knew the sound was coming from her GeoPort. It was working! The chirping meant that her GeoPort had recharged and was ready to Warp again. She yanked the unit out of her pocket, ready to punch in 23.1483° N, 79.9015° E, the longitude and latitude numbers for the Konanavlah Sun Temple, but she saw something strange. There was already a set of numbers flashing across the unit.

21.52, 75.3, 78.14, 0.9786

Daisha knew instantly the numbers weren't latitude and longitude. She rattled her brain, trying to figure out what they were.

"Where did they come from?" she whispered to herself.

"What are you mumbling about?" Loosha asked.

She ignored her captor and tried to erase the

numbers and type in the coordinates for the Sun Temple. It didn't work. The numbers were stuck in place.

"What's wrong with this thing?" she wondered aloud.

"Give me that," Loosha growled, reaching for the GeoPort. "The Doctor might give me a bonus for this."

Daisha pulled the unit away. "Get away from me!" she screamed in his face.

Loosha grabbed Daisha by the arm. Daisha countered his move by punching him in the stomach.

"Owww!" Loosha cried out.

Daisha pushed him away, but he quickly recovered and snatched her by the wrist. Just as he was about to take the GeoPort from her hands, she pressed the SW button. With a blast of white smoke and electrical discharge, both of them detonated into the Warp.

Chapter Five
MUNI

Muni parted her office window curtains and stared outside. A melancholy smile stretched across her face. She loved watching the children play in the grass of the Antakaale's Sri Lankan tea plantation, but this scene made her sad too. She and her followers used to have eight children. Now they were down to seven, all of them girls between the ages of three and a half and six. Her thoughts swam with memories of the other child who was no longer with the group. Varya was her name—one of the Sanskrit words meaning "precious." At twelve months, she had just learned to toddle. Her big toothy smile and thick black hair had always delighted Muni.

But now she was gone and so was her mother. This was not acceptable, and three of Muni's most loyal devotees were at this very moment hunting them down.

A knock came at the door.

"Come in," Muni said, still staring out the window.

Pavana, her young assistant, came into the room. Like all women of the Antakaale—a Sanskrit term meaning "the end of life"—she had the group's sign tattooed in the center of her forehead, a unalome and lotus symbol inside a yellow sun.

"I have good news," Pavana said, setting down a pitcher of iced tea.

Muni turned from the window. "About Gita and Varya?" she asked.

"Sorry?"

"Varya—the child," Muni repeated, a little louder this time. Her Polish accent always became thicker and harder to understand the more excited she became.

"Yes. We've recovered both of them. They've just arrived now."

Relief washed over Muni. She lifted her head to the sky and mouthed the words *thank you.*

"Where'd they find them?" she asked.

"Negombo fishing village," Pavana answered. "Evidently, she was caught while begging one of the locals to sail her and the child across the sea to Kanyakumari."

Muni shook her head in disgust. "They wouldn't

have lasted a day sailing in one of those rickety boats. If she weren't such a superstar in geophysics, I'd have taken the child and let her drift at sea. What was Gita's name before she came to us?"

Pavana tapped her chin, thinking. "Luciana Lopez, I believe."

"Yes, I think you're correct. I was so thrilled when she heard the Voices and joined me."

Muni poured herself a glass of iced tea, lit a stick of cinnamon incense, and again looked out the window. This time her gaze wasn't on the children, but at a large, ancient Buddha statue amid temple ruins sitting adjacent to their property. The temple had housed several female Buddhist monks. Yet another sign from the Voices that only women belonged among the Antakaale. They were all her precious daughters, and she loved them deeply.

"We need to get her back on our side," Muni said, closing the window's curtains. "Besides you and me, she's the only other scientist we have among us."

Pavana nodded. "And a brilliant one at that."

"Take me to her."

Muni fluffed her long silver hair, slipped a fresh lotus flower behind her ear, and draped a white prayer shawl over her shoulders. She and Pavana shuffled outside, barefoot. They walked down a long dirt path, past the rows of wooden huts perched on stilts that housed her followers. A warm late-morning breeze blew through the rolling hills. Green fields of tea cultivation, the Antakaale's main source of income, stretched as far as the eye could see.

"She's in there," Pavana said, pointing toward a small bunker with a heavy steel door.

A woman stood guard. Like Pavana, she was young with long hair parted down the middle and the Antakaale symbol tattooed to her forehead.

"Has she made a fuss?" Muni asked.

The woman shook her head. "No. She's been very quiet but refused fresh water and food."

Muni smirked. "Another one bent on a hunger strike. Open the door."

The door creaked open, and Muni stepped inside. Pavana attempted to follow.

"I want to speak to her alone," Muni said. "Wait outside."

Muni squinted in the squalid darkness, waiting for her eyes to adjust to the dim light. When her pupils had properly dilated, she saw Gita sitting in the corner. There was blood on her forehead as though she had been trying to rub away the Antakaale tattoo.

"Where's my baby?" Gita said, her voice weak.

"Varya is in good hands," Muni answered.

"Her name isn't Varya," Gita spit out. "It's Catalina, and we want to go home."

"My dear, you and the baby *are* home."

Gita launched into a dry, hacking cough.

Muni produced a water bottle from her pocket and handed it to her. "Drink this."

"I don't want anything from you," Gita said, throwing the bottle across the room.

"You're dehydrated. Death comes quickly to those who don't drink."

Gita lowered her head and sobbed into her hands for several minutes. Muni stared at her, beads of sweat dripping from her temples and down her wrinkled face.

"You and Varya couldn't have made it to India in one of those death traps," Muni said when Gita's crying had run its course. "Is it so bad here?"

"I never should have left my professorship," Gita said, her voice barely above a whisper. "I want to go back. This was a mistake."

"The only mistake you made was leaving us in the first place. You're an extremely educated woman. What were you possibly thinking?"

"That I wanted my baby and me to get out of here."

"The Voices are calling to you. Don't you want a seat at the table of New Earth?"

"The Voices aren't real. I want to see Catalina."

A knock came at the door.

"Not yet," Muni said.

Pavana's muffled voice echoed from behind the door. "But it's very important. You'll want to hear this right away."

Muni knelt down and stroked Gita's sweaty, knotted hair. "You'll see Varya again," she said. "And you'll realize what a mistake you made. The Voices delivered you to us. I need you, Gita. We'll never make it to New Earth without you."

There was another knock on the door, this time more urgent than before.

"I won't force you to take water," Muni said. "But if you don't drink very soon, you may not live to see Varya again anyway."

The door opened, and Muni slipped outside into the bright light.

Chapter Six
AXEL

Charu's skill at *Aadu puli aatam*, or Game of Goats and Tigers, was legendary in the caves. In the game, one player assumed the role of the goat. The other was the tiger. The purpose for the tiger was to hunt the goats and for the goat to try to block the tiger's movements.

"I only need to ambush one more of your goats and I win," Axel said.

"Don't be too confident," Charu said. "I've already taken out two of your tigers. One more and *I* win." She gave him a sly grin. "That would make twenty-three victories for me, *zero* for you. I've been keeping track."

Axel smirked at her. They had been playing the game to pass the time as his wound healed. He carefully studied the board and moved his tiger into position.

"Is that your final move?" Charu asked.

"Yes," Axel said confidently.

"Absolutely one hundred percent sure? I'll let you take it back."

"I'm so sure that if this were chess, I'd say 'checkmate.' But I guess in this game we say 'check goat.'"

Charu rolled her eyes and moved a game piece. With a flick of her finger, Axel's tiger flew off the board. "Game over," she said. "I'm still the undisputed, undefeated, all-world *Aadu puli aatam* champion."

"No way!" Axel cried out. "My tiger had you cornered!"

"Better luck next time, my friend. And like the old proverb says: *When a tiger is in trouble, even a goat will kick him.*"

"What's that supposed to mean?"

"I have no idea," Charu said. "But it seems appropriate in this situation."

Axel laughed. "One more game. I'll beat you this time."

Kundan stepped into the room. He was carrying a first-aid kit in one hand and a bottle of antiseptic with the other.

"How badly did she beat you?" he asked.

"The game came down to the wire," Charu said. "Axel is getting much better."

"I hope you're not going to use more of that cleaning junk on my cut," Axel said with a pained grimace. "The stuff stings like a jellyfish. And having been stung by one, I know what I'm talking about."

"You must mean the mixture of ethanol and hydrogen peroxide in the solution," Kundan said. "These ingredients activate receptors in the body that trigger a burning feeling."

"Whatever," Axel said. "All I know is that it hurts."

Charu lit the torch hanging on the wall. The room glowed much brighter. Kundan ordered Axel to lie down on the cot. He rolled up Axel's baggy pants, which Charu jokingly called his *punjammies*, and carefully cleaned the wound.

"That wasn't so bad, was it?" Kundan asked, applying a fresh bandage.

"Actually, the sting didn't hurt like usual."

Kundan slipped the cap back on the bottle of antiseptic. "That's because you're healing. It's only been a couple days, so I'd say you have another two weeks before the stitches start to dissolve."

Axel stood up, shuffled to a side table, and poured a glass of water. He was able to walk now with only a slight limp, even if it was only to go to the bathroom in the chamber pot, which he thought was the most disgusting thing in the world.

A pang of guilt made his stomach gurgle and neck

muscles tense. Here he was playing board games with Charu while Daisha was gone. He had no idea where she was or what would come next. How would he ever make it out of this cave to search for her?

"Where's Megan?" Axel asked. "I need to see her."

Charu shot Kundan a concerned glance. "She's not in the caves," she said.

"What do you mean *not in the caves*?" Axel asked.

"She and Jag went up top to check their iPhones because there's no cellular service down here," Kundan said. And then he left the room.

Axel scratched gently at his wound as Charu grabbed a spray bottle from a shelf. She started watering down the dirt floor, a practice she did every day to keep the dust down. Daisha once again flitted through his thoughts.

Was she alive?

If so, where was she?

Why did all of this happen?

He quickly pushed the thoughts away—just thinking about her made tears form at the corners of his eyes.

"I need to get out of this room and wander around a bit," Axel said. "I'm starting to feel a little claustrophobic."

"I think that will be okay," Charu said, putting back

the spray bottle. "I'll show you where I stay. My room isn't nearly as extravagant as yours."

Axel grunted. "If you think this is extravagant, then you must live inside a rat hole."

Charu guided him into a dimly lit passageway. The smells of sweet, smoky incense and a warm clay pot filled with jasmine rice filled his nostrils. Axel hobbled along, gazing at the murals and carvings covering the rock walls. From what Jag had told him, the artwork was more than three thousand years old and in a near perfect state of preservation.

"All of this wonder is thanks to the cave's hidden location," Jag had said. "The vandals do not know of it, and the natural elements have not eroded the stone or faded the colors."

They passed the giant four-armed-man statue and several other elegant carvings before Charu turned down a much narrower passageway. They scooted past a series of cave openings, all of which were covered with colorful beaded curtains.

"This is where I sleep," Charu said as she parted the beads.

The cave was huge. Several lit candles bathed the space in a murky golden glow. Hindu-themed tapestries covered the walls. Several cots, the same as his, lined the floors. All of them were unmade except one.

"I'm the only one left," Charu offered.

"What do you mean?" Axel asked.

"The other female dancers fled when the Sun Temple began to implode. They went home."

"What made you stay?"

"I didn't want to go back to my parents in Bhopal. The caves were the only other place to go when the Temple started crumbling."

"What are your parents like?" Axel asked.

"They are devout Hindus. It seems like they think since I'm a temple dancer it will give them extra points in the afterlife or something."

"What do you want to do?" asked Axel.

"I want to study physics at the Indian School of Science in Bangalore," said Charu. "Either that or be a movie star like Kangana Ranaut. Did you see her in *Tanu Weds Manu*? It's my all-time favorite film."

Axel smiled. "Sorry, I missed that one. Seriously. You should talk to Megan. She has a PhD in physics."

Charu's eyes lit up. "Really?"

"Yes, really. Why don't you just go to school and study physics for yourself?"

"Because my parents won't pay," she said in a low, sad voice. "It's very expensive. However, they gladly paid for my older brother to go to engineering college."

"Why don't they pay for you too?"

"They're old-fashioned. In their world, boys go to college and girls have arranged marriages. They have a boy already picked out for me, but I don't like him and never will."

Charu opened her nightstand drawer and pulled out something small and round.

"This is your thing," she said.

"What are you talking about?" Axel wondered, not quite seeing what was in her hand because of the dim light.

"When you arrived, this fell out of your pocket. Remember, you picked it up and hurled it across the room? You said you never wanted to see it again. I saved it just in case you changed your mind."

Charu handed him Daisha's GeoPort. Axel rolled the unit over in his palms. The thing was still dead. Its pulses of blue starbursts and flashing latitude and longitude coordinates were gone. For more than six months, the GeoPort had been his lifeline to Daisha, an invisible, solar wind-fueled cord that connected them together.

Axel frantically pressed the SW button on his GeoPort, hoping it would magically turn on and lead him to Daisha.

"This needs to work!" Axel groaned in frustration.

"And you need to calm down," Charu ordered. "I don't want your stitches to tear open."

"Come on!" Axel pleaded. "Turn on and send me into the Warp!"

There was nothing. No burning electrical smell, loud boom, or discharge of white smoke. He was still in an underground cave somewhere in the Indian jungle. And he might never see Daisha again.

Chapter Seven
DAISHA

Daisha ripped through the Warp at breakneck speed. A kaleidoscope of colors flickered before her eyes. Vivid images appeared on the pulsing artery walls. She saw ocean waves crashing against the shore, giant tortoises laying eggs in the sand, green iguanas scurrying in tall grass, and flocks of colorful birds soaring through the sky.

A blazing beam of divine white light appeared in the distance.

"The sun," Daisha whispered.

And just like the light that had appeared when the Warp had swept her away from Axel at the Konanavlah Sun Temple, this brightness was soft, kind, and peaceful. It was nothing like the blistering sun back on Earth.

She hurtled directly toward the light, so entranced by its serene beauty that she hadn't felt Loosha's presence soaring directly beside her.

The sun faded away like a giant eclipse in time-lapse. Everything went black as Daisha and Loosha spiraled downward through the nothingness. Hot air blasted her in the face, and her ears popped from the sudden drop in elevation. Fuzzy images began to take shape below. Just as they were about to crash-land, a soft pillow of air encased them moments before impact.

Daisha landed on hard, packed dirt. The impact jarred her bones, like a linebacker had plowed into her. She sat up on her hands and knees. Her head was spinning, stomach churning. Loosha was lying next her, vomiting.

"What just happened?" Loosha stammered between dry heaves.

"We went through the Warp," Daisha said. "You know what that's like. You and your fellow goons were chasing Axel and me for six months through the thing."

"Our trips were nothing like that. It was only a big black void. I just saw the most beautiful thing in the world. The lights, colors, pictures. Like being part of a beautiful painting...though, the feeling at the end is the same."

Daisha wiped grit from her eyes, regained her

balance, and stood up. She was standing on a well-worn path in a lush, green jungle. A scent of decomposing leaves mixed with exotic flowers wafted in her nostrils. Colorful birds she had never seen before flitted among the tree branches. Several mosquitoes swarmed her head, their incessant whine echoing in her ears.

"I've been here before!" she exclaimed, swatting at the bloodsuckers. "We've landed back in India!"

"What are you talking about?" Loosha asked, still on his hands and knees, face flush from throwing up.

Daisha looked down, sneered, and kicked him directly in the ribs. Loosha cried out in pain as she sprinted down the path. It was a perfect time for her to escape.

Thick vines and barbed bushes tugged at her skin and clothes as she ran through the jungle. She came to a clearing and stopped for a second, scanning the horizon, hoping to see the golden crown of the Konanavlah Sun Temple poking above the canopy of trees.

"Axel!" she hollered. "I'm here! It's Daisha! Where are you?"

Footsteps pounded from behind. She turned and saw Loosha coming for her. Before she took another step, the man had reached her.

"Stop!" Loosha ordered, grabbing her roughly by the arm. "Don't ever run from me again!"

Daisha ripped her arm away from his grasp. "Why don't you just let me go!" she spit. "I just want to find Axel—that's all!"

"What do you know?" said Loosha. "I want to find him too. He might still be worth some more *pieniądze*. But do you really want to be alone out here in the middle of nowhere?"

Daisha didn't care much about being left alone. But Loosha did have a point. Maybe he could help her find Axel. And it wasn't like he was going to hurt her—Loosha would want her in one piece when he delivered her to the Doctor. So no matter how annoying Loosha was, it was probably in her best interest to stay with him for the time being and then make her escape when they were close to finding Axel.

"Fine," Daisha said, shaking his hand off her arm.

"How do you know we're in India?" Loosha asked.

"Because—" Daisha started to say, but a large wooden sign made her voice stick in her throat.

The sign said *Parque Nacional Galápagos, Isla de Isabela, Ecuador.*

A tear rolled down Daisha's cheek.

"Why are you crying?" Loosha asked. "What does that sign say?"

"It's Spanish for 'Galápagos National Park, Isabela

Island, Ecuador.' That means we're not in India, and Axel's not here."

Daisha turned and continued down the path with Loosha close behind. She didn't know what to do, but she knew she didn't want to be in the middle of nowhere come nightfall.

They walked for several hours, eating wild red berries that tasted like a slightly sweeter version of cherry tomatoes. The whole time, pangs of fear clenched her stomach. Warp travel wasn't supposed to work this way. *She* was the one who typed in the coordinates and flew away, not the other way around. Never once in her six months of using the GeoPort did numbers pop up by themselves. Besides, she and Axel had destroyed the permanent X-Point, and that should have ended Geographical Transportation altogether.

As the sun disappeared over the horizon, Daisha and Loosha made it to the ocean. Half the beach was dark volcanic sand. The other half was light beige. Across the bay, they saw the burning lights of a large village.

"At least we're close to civilization," Loosha said. "Tomorrow we'll go there. I have lots of money."

"Who's going to take care of Boris?" Daisha wondered aloud. "When we Warped, he was still locked in that room."

"The Doctor has many domestic employees. They'll feed him."

Loosha slipped off his canvas belt and used it to tie Daisha's wrist to his.

"I'm going to sleep now," he said, tying the knot tight. "Try anything funny and I'll know." He reclined in the sand, yawned, and closed his eyes.

Daisha tried to stay awake, but it was a losing battle. Her eyelids fluttered and her head bobbed. As she was about to drift off, confusing thoughts popped into her half-awake, half-dreaming mind.

How did Loosha go through the Warp with me when only my DNA makes the GeoPort work? He grabbed me right before I pressed the Satellite Warp button. Maybe if another living form is touching me they also teleport. I guess this is another quirk my mom and Axel's dad didn't know about Warp travel. I wonder what other things about the GeoPort I don't know.

* * *

Daisha and Loosha awoke the next morning to the sound of a loud siren coming from the village. They sat up, rubbed their eyes, and saw three Ecuadorian men frantically pulling log canoes out of the water. Three boys of around ten years old ran up the beach carrying fishing poles.

"Hey, you!" Loosha shouted at them. "What's going on?"

"Tsunami warning!" one of the boys hollered, his eyes wide with fear.

Loosha looked at Daisha. "What's he talking about?"

Daisha stood up and untied the belt around her wrist. "I think he said there's going to be a tsunami."

"Tsunami? As in a giant wave?" Loosha asked.

"That's what the kid said."

Loosha pointed to the water. "Holy crap!" he cried. "Look at that!"

Daisha glanced at the shore. The ocean was receding dramatically, like someone had pulled a plug. A loud rumble rattled the palm trees.

"Something's not right," she said.

The entire horizon began to swell with water. A giant wave emerged in the distance, gaining height and power as it rolled toward the shore.

"*Correr por la tierra alta!*" screamed one of the old men who had been pulling his canoe from the water. "*Correr!*"

"What's he screaming?" Loosha asked.

"*Correr* means 'run' in Spanish," Daisha said. "We better take his advice."

They turned around and raced through the jungle.

The old men had fallen behind, but the three kids were well ahead of them. Several panicked people emerged from the trees, running for their lives. Screams echoed along the beach. Daisha looked over her shoulder and saw the wave violently pound the shore. The surge of water clawed its way inland, toppling trees and washing away hummocks and hillsides. Just as the floodwater was about to sweep them away, the GeoPort began to chirp.

Daisha looked down and saw the same four sets of numbers flashing across the screen.

21.52, 75.3, 78.14, 0.9786

"Where are these numbers coming from?" Daisha cried out in frustration. "And how can we Warp? It hasn't been twenty-four hours."

Loosha grabbed her arm. "It doesn't matter. Get us into the Warp or we're dead!"

Daisha pressed the SW button, and both of them blasted into the abyss.

Chapter Eight
MUNI

Muni stepped out of the bunker, shielding her eyes from the intense sun. The smoky scent of tea leaves roasting in processing huts wafted in the air.

"Look at this news flash on my phone," Pavana said.

"Not now," Muni said. "We need to assemble everybody in the Temple."

"Why?"

"Questions about Gita will start popping up. I need to give them an explanation, plus a little reminder of the Voices and our destiny."

Pavana nodded and took off down the path. Muni headed in the opposite direction, toward the far end of the property. After a brisk ten-minute walk, she arrived at a large, open-air structure made from bamboo and palm leaves. Several yoga mats lined the floor. A stone altar etched with the Antakaale's sign sat prominently at the head of the Temple. A large bronze gong stood off to the right.

Muni stood at the altar, reliving the glorious moment when she first heard the Voices more than twenty years ago. She had just accepted the Vetlesen Prize, the geophysics version of the Nobel Prize, for her work on global warming, when the sky parted and the Voices spoke directly to her. The Voices weren't people, but powerful spheres of psychic energy, swirling globes of sunshine that descended directly into her mind. Their message was so profound and spiritually penetrating she gave up everything to fulfill their message.

We are not of this Earth and neither are you. Destroy Old Earth and save humankind from the evil of itself. Only the hallowed female holds the key to New Earth. Bountiful peace awaits all women who believe.

These were the first words the Voices whispered into her ear. Muni knew without a doubt that *hallowed female* meant only women would gain entrance to New Earth, and only women could become Antakaale. The Voices' teachings came fast and furious after that, and she assembled them all in a slim book of ninety-nine pages titled *The Way to New Earth*.

The one-time Benedykta Wójcik, PhD, esteemed Caltech professor of geophysics, became Muni, a name she selected from Sanskrit that meant "thinker" or "sage." She quickly abandoned her life's work and tossed away all of the accompanying awards. Her ex-husband, an American geologist named Russell Hollinger, gained full custody of their daughter and moved away. She had long ago forgotten about him, but her little *córka* was never far from her thoughts.

The girl was four the last time Muni had seen her. She would be in her mid-twenties by now, perhaps a graduate student in science herself.

"I will see you again one day, my sweet *córka*," Muni whispered, choking back emotion. "And you will come to hear the Voices."

The first of her followers stepped into the Temple, ripping Muni from her thoughts. Soon, all eighty-seven women of the Antakaale filled the Temple. They sat down cross-legged on the yoga mats as they did every day for the morning meditation. Those who were mothers held children in their laps. In accordance with the Voices' teachings, Muni allowed only mothers and daughters among the group. She had turned away many women with sons who wanted to join.

Utter joy filled Muni's heart as she gazed at her followers with her penetrating, hypnotic green eyes. They had come from different parts of the world: France,

Ireland, England, Vietnam, Canada, Brazil, Australia, Somalia, Syria, the United States, and one spotty teenager from Iceland.

Some were doctors, lawyers, college professors, secretaries, police officers, and elementary schoolteachers in previous lives. Others were housewives and still others students. Some were retired. Now, they were all Antakaale, working on the tea plantation, passing the time while awaiting passage to New Earth.

Muni picked up the ceremonial mallet and pounded the gong three times. The sound rang out, its powerful vibrations bouncing off the bamboo and echoing in their ears.

"My daughters," Muni said with a huge smile. "How I love each and every one of you." She held out her arms as if giving them an embrace. "The Voices have chosen *me* to show *you* the way to freedom, peace, and eternal life. There is no other way but that of the Voices."

"No other way but that of the Voices," the worshippers repeated in almost zombie-like devotion. Even the children seemed taken by Muni's message.

"The time of our departure to New Earth is not yet upon us," Muni explained. "I have assembled you here today as a reminder of our mission and daily devotion. As my advisors and I plot our way, we must not forget verse number ten of the Voices' teachings. Patience is the greatest gift along the path toward New Earth."

Her followers chanted, "Patience is the greatest gift."

"Now, I must ask you a question. Do you see Gita?"

Everyone shook their heads.

"Our lovely Gita is no longer with us," Muni continued, "because she has been attacked by the Soul Worms."

Cries of anguish, fear, and pain filled the temple. People sobbed as others tried to comfort them.

"Is she okay?" someone asked.

"I want to help her," chimed another.

"Gita's fate is up to the Voices now," Muni said. "But remember our beloveds' warning about the Soul Worms in the sacred texts. They want nothing more than to deafen our ears to the Voices."

"They want to deafen our ears to the Voices," the crowd answered back.

Muni banged the gong again, this time louder than before. "We are vulnerable to attack when we let doubt creep into our frail human minds," she preached. "They have even caused our dear Gita to try and scratch the blessed mark from her forehead. Bring me her child!"

A tall Somali woman named Faraw emerged from the crowd carrying the toddler. She handed Varya to

Muni. The little girl's thumb plopped into her mouth as her head rested on Muni's chest.

"New Earth belongs to this precious daughter and *all* who believe," Muni said.

A chorus erupted from the crowd.

"We believe! We believe! We believe!"

Muni joined the chant as she walked into the audience with Varya in her arms. Her followers fell to their knees and wept with joy as she walked out of the Temple and down a dirt path toward her office.

Chapter Nine
AXEL

A hopeless sense of dread filled Axel's heart. He needed a working GeoPort to find Daisha. For all he knew, she might be alive and waiting for him back at Hoover Park Dog Run.

"I'd give anything for this to work again!" Axel hollered.

"You're scaring me," Charu said. "Are you getting cave fever?"

Axel held up the GeoPort for her. "Didn't Jag or Megan tell you what this is used for?"

Charu shook her head.

"It's a GeoPort," Axel explained. "That's short for Geographical Transportation. My dad and Daisha's mom invented the process. I can travel anywhere in the world with this thing at the press of a button. That is, I *used* to be able to."

A confused look washed over Charu's face. "This can't be real," she said. "It sounds like something out of an episode of *Badi Door Se Aaye Hain*."

"What's Baddee door see ya...or however you pronounce it."

"*Badi Door Se Aaye Hain* means 'come from far away' in Hindi. It's a very funny science fiction show about a family of aliens who crash-land their spaceship in the middle of the jungle."

"This isn't science fiction. A GeoPort is science fact."

Axel told Charu about the crazy events that had led up to him being at the temple when it exploded.

"I'm sorry to hear about your father," Charu said, her eyes misty from the story. "As for this Doctor person, Earth provides enough to satisfy every man's need but not every man's greed."

"That's pretty deep," Axel said. "Did you just make it up?"

"I wish," Charu said. "It's a quote from Mahatma Gandhi."

"I know about Gandhi. We learned a little about him in history class, the British occupation of India and everything. You know, I even voted *yes* at school to officially change the name of Columbus Day to Gandhi Day."

Charu gave him a blank look. "Never mind, it's not important. May I see it?"

Axel handed the GeoPort over. "Sure. Maybe you can get it to work."

Charu studied the unit, rubbing it with her fingers. "Strange that this Doctor tried to kill you just to get this particular GeoPort. Why doesn't he just make one for himself?"

"Because making money is the only thing that scumbag's good for. He needs people a lot smarter than him to make one of these babies. So far, he hasn't found anyone as intelligent as my dad or Daisha's mom."

A female voice echoed off the rock walls outside in the hallway.

"Axel? Charu?"

"It's Megan!" Axel said.

Charu helped Axel shuffle into the passage. They hurried down a corridor and saw Megan standing in front of Axel's room.

"Hey!" Megan called out, running toward him.

"Where's Jag?" Charu asked.

"Looking for Larraj," Megan answered. "No one can seem to find him."

"What were you doing out of the caves?" Axel asked. "Did you see any Pursuers?"

Megan shook her head. "None of them, thankfully. Jag and I spent our time wandering around the rock shelter like tourists until we picked up cell service. I've been scouring the news for any information about the Doctor, the Sun Temple, and anything else we could discover."

"Did you find anything out?" asked Axel.

"Well, for starters, the Doctor's in big trouble."

"Good," Axel said with a smile. "I hope they throw the book at the jerk."

"There also have been three major earthquakes and a devastating tsunami around the globe in the last forty-eight hours. One of the quakes was centered close to our hometown of Palo Alto. The tsunami nearly wiped out the Galápagos Islands."

Axel's mouth dropped open. "Was the earthquake bad back home?"

"Bad enough to destroy a lot of buildings, but only three reported deaths so far, thank goodness."

"Hopefully one of those buildings was Hatch Enterprises, LLC. Do you think what's happening around the world has anything to do with what happened back at the Sun Temple?"

Megan shrugged. "Don't know for sure. But it's a very odd coincidence. There's no doubt you and Daisha destroyed the permanent X-Point back there."

Axel took the GeoPort from Charu and handed it to Megan. "Can you figure out a way to get this thing to work?"

Megan clutched the GeoPort and paced the hall. She narrowed her eyes, biting her bottom lip, deep in thought. Axel could almost see the billions of neurons firing inside her brain. He had watched his father perform the same ritual many times when trying to decipher an advanced physics equation.

"Professors Jack and Tandala let me in on almost every aspect of Geographical Transportation, but not everything," Megan said after several moments. "All this news makes me remember something very strange your dad and Daisha's mom told me literally the day before they—"

Megan didn't have to finish her sentence. Axel knew she had cut off the words *were killed* so as not to hurt his feelings.

"What did they tell you?" Axel asked.

"That they were still studying the long-term effects of X-Points and were unsure of what would happen if one were destroyed."

"What's an X-Point again?" Charu asked.

"X-Points, also called electron diffusion regions,

are places in Earth's magnetic field that connect to the sun's magnetic field," Megan explained. "To make a long story short, it's the power that makes Axel's GeoPort transport him to any place in the world within seconds."

Charu looked at Axel, her eyes wide with excitement. "Now *that's* why I want to go to college and study physics."

Megan smiled at her and then turned back to Axel. "Your dad took me aside and told me if something went wrong I might have to get help."

"What kind of help?" Axel asked.

"That's the cryptic part. I don't know what kind of help he meant. He knew the potential downsides of destroying a permanent X-Point, but they had to make a choice."

"Either let the Doctor rule the world by getting his grubby hands on the technology," Axel said, "or destroy the permanent X-Point without being certain what side effects it might have."

"I know they made the right decision," Megan said. "But it seems like those 'side effects' might be pretty serious if we don't do something."

"Then it seems we have to make a *new* X-Point," Charu said.

"You're a smart girl," Megan told Charu. "I think that's exactly what we need to do."

"How in the world are we supposed to create a new X-Point?" Axel wondered.

"I have no idea," Megan answered. "We need to get Larraj and Jag's advice."

Axel tossed his hands up in exasperation. "So those two guys suddenly have advanced degrees in astrophysics?" he said sarcastically.

"No, but they have advanced degrees in the palm leaf prophecies," Charu offered, reaching up to touch Axel's shoulder to calm him down. "They know many things from the past and future."

Axel cupped Charu's hand and sighed. "You're right. They sure knew all about Daisha and me, and predicted what would happen at the Sun Temple."

"Exactly," Megan said. "If you would've told me a month ago that I'd be in India gathering scientific conclusions from a five-thousand-year-old strip of a palm leaf, I'd have called you crazy. But Larraj and Jag were dead right about the Sun Temple, so they may know what we have to do now."

"Then let's go ask them," Axel said. "I can't take one more day of not knowing what happened to Daisha."

Charu grabbed a torch from the wall, and the three of them scurried down the hall toward Jag's chamber.

Chapter Ten
DAISHA

Daisha exploded out of thin air and landed on hard gravel. She sat up on one knee and took slow, deep breaths. Loosha was lying a few yards away on his back. His complexion was ten shades of green from their blast through the Warp. But at least this time he wasn't blowing chunks.

"Where are we?" Loosha asked.

"Not the Galápagos Islands, that's for sure," Daisha answered.

Hot, bright sunshine beat down on her, and for a heart-pumping second, she thought she might be blasting directly toward the sun again. Stunning, towering red rock formations surrounded them. The sky was perfectly blue and cloudless. The smell of wet stone and sweet sage wafted in the air. A middle-aged man and woman were standing next to a set of coin-operated binoculars.

"What in the world was that?" the woman asked, a shocked expression on her face.

"How dare you light a firecracker off in a state park," the man said with a scowl. "I should report you to a warden, but they're probably headed this way after hearing a bang like that."

Daisha stood up, ignoring the man and woman. They had landed at some kind of scenic lookout. A sign read RED ROCK STATE PARK.

"Where's Red Rock State Park?" Daisha asked.

"Sedona, Arizona," the man barked. "Are you two so out of it you don't even know where you are?"

"Shut up and get out of here," Loosha said, wiping sweat from his forehead.

"Don't you tell me to shut up," the man retorted.

Loosha stood up. His eyes narrowed, making his already menacing presence even scarier. The man slowly backed away. He took one look at the pistol holstered to Loosha's side and hurried his wife back down the trail.

Daisha looked down at the GeoPort. The numbers 21.52, 75.3, 78.14, 0.9786 flashed on the screen. "I need to figure you out," she said.

"What are you mumbling?" Loosha asked.

"The numbers on my GeoPort aren't latitude and longitude. Plus, the Warp's supposed to take twenty-four hours to reset, but for some weird reason it's happening sooner now."

"Big deal."

"It's a *big deal*, all right."

"Give me that thing," Loosha said. "I want to go back to Palo Alto."

"Then you better start walking," Daisha said.

Loosha grabbed Daisha's arm and snatched away the GeoPort.

"I want that back!" she cried.

"Tell me how it works," Loosha demanded.

Daisha reared back to lash out at him, but quickly realized *she* was now the one in charge.

"The GeoPort's useless to you," Daisha said. "My mom and Axel's dad designed it to work only with *my* DNA."

"Then how did *I* go through the Warp with you?" Loosha asked.

"Because..." Daisha started to say. "I don't know. Something weird is happening."

An angry grimace washed over Loosha's face. "Don't lie to me!" he roared. "I want to go back to Palo Alto. Now!"

Daisha grabbed the GeoPort from his hands and started manically pressing buttons.

"See!" she hollered back. "It's frozen!"

Two girls and a boy emerged from the trail. They were young, college-aged, and loaded with backpacks. The boy was as tall as Loosha, but not nearly as muscled and tough looking. One girl had long blond hair pulled back into a ponytail and was wearing a University of Arizona T-shirt. The other, a Hispanic girl, had thick black hair and big dark eyes.

The boy plopped a quarter into one of the coin-operated binoculars. "This is so beautiful," he said with awe.

"Let me see," the blond girl said, nudging the boy aside. "Magnificent."

"My turn," the dark-eyed girl said.

While the college kids took turns looking through the binoculars, Loosha and Daisha huddle around an information kiosk.

"What happens now?" Loosha asked.

"We wait," Daisha answered.

"For what?"

Daisha rolled her eyes. "Oh my gosh! Don't you get it by now? If the GeoPort is working and the Warp is up and running properly, it takes twenty-four hours to reset. Don't you listen?"

A sheepish look washed over Loosha's face. "But I

didn't think we were in the Galápagos for that long before we Warped away," he said.

"Right. That's why I said if the Warp is running *properly*," Daisha responded. "But with you Warping with me, us Warping early, and earthquakes and tsunamis following us wherever we go, I would say the Warp is definitely not working *properly*."

As the meaning of the words sunk in, a look Daisha had never seen before passed over Loosha's face. For the first time, she saw his tough exterior melt ever so slightly and be replaced with the emotion that must have been written all over her own face: fear.

It was quiet for a moment and Daisha realized the college kids were no longer chatting. She looked and saw they were now eyeing her and Loosha. The boy was staring at the pistol holstered to Loosha's side with an uneasy look on his face.

"Where does this trail lead?" Daisha asked, breaking the tension.

The dark-eyed girl pointed back to where they had come from. "That way goes back to the visitor center," she said.

"Apache Fire Trail's just ahead," the blond girl added.

"Is there camping?" Loosha asked.

The boy shook his head. "You're not allowed to camp

in the park. But there are lots of campgrounds outside the park boundaries."

The sound of clomping horse hooves captured their attention. They looked up and saw two men, high in the saddle and wearing Smokey the Bear hats, riding up the trail from the visitor center.

"Here come some park rangers," the blond girl said. "You can probably ask them about the best place to camp."

"Do you think that old couple reported us?" Daisha asked Loosha.

"Maybe. Maybe not," Loosha said. "But I don't want to take any chances. Let's go."

They ran down a path into the heart of the red rocks. The trail twisted and turned between juniper and mesquite trees. As the men on horseback drew closer, Daisha and Loosha veered off the trail and skittered down a rocky slope full of prickly pear and other kinds of cacti. The sound of rushing water filled their ears. A large creek came into view.

"We'll hide along the bank," Loosha said. "When the Warp resets, we go back to Palo Alto."

Loosha stood guard as Daisha sandwiched herself between two large boulders. They waited for hours, until the sun set and darkness fell over the red rocks. She thought of the random numbers that had appeared on the GeoPort. Not just how they got there, but why they were there in the first place. Were they guiding her to Axel? If it happened again, would Axel be waiting for her at the next place? And why did the GeoPort send her to Red Rock State Park in Sedona, Arizona? The place was beautiful, but why here? These questions tumbled in her mind as she drifted into a restless, dreamless sleep.

Chapter Eleven
MUNI

Varya was fast asleep when Muni made it back to her office. The warm feel of the little girl pressed against her chest made Muni's heart swell with happiness. All the daughters were special to her, but she loved Varya the most—from the thumb sucking to the big toothy smile and the way she always twirled her hair.

She gently laid Varya down on a mound of soft pillows. The child stirred for a moment and fell back asleep. A flitter near the open window caught her attention. An Indian paradise flycatcher had landed on the sill. The bird's sapphire-colored head, white chest, and bright orange wings and tail feathers were unmistakable. Her nest cradling four speckled eggs was just outside the window in the low-hanging branches of a Ruk tree.

Pavana burst into the office. "You have to see this," she said.

"Shhhh," Muni hushed, pressing a finger to her lips. "Our angel is sleeping. The Voices may be using dreams to speak to her."

Pavana handed Muni her cell phone. "Look at this."

"What's this about?" Muni asked, her voice barely above a whisper.

"It's a newsflash from Huri News. I thought it might interest you."

Muni looked at the screen. The words *Indian Sun Temple explosion…American held for questioning* scrolled across the screen. She tapped the link with her finger and read the brief article.

Officials in the Indian state of Odisha have detained American billionaire Doctor Lennon Hatch over an explosion at the ancient Konanavlah Sun Temple. Eyewitness reports say the American had surrounded the temple with several pieces of scientific equipment and caused a serious explosion. Damage to the temple is unknown. Odisha State Police are holding Doctor Hatch and several of his associates for questioning.

The eight-hundred-year-old shrine is a major tourist attraction and considered one of the most revered sites in all of India.

"Hatch?" Muni said, a hint of surprised shock in her voice. "What in the world was that man doing in India?"

"Do you know this person?"

"I met him years ago when I was a geophysics professor at Caltech."

"If he's a doctor of geophysics then why don't I know about him?"

"He's *not* a doctor. The man's a multibillionaire who had once funded a couple of my former colleagues."

"Was this before or after you had won the Vetlesen Prize?"

"Well before. The man was money hungry and thought science was the way to even more wealth. I wanted nothing to do with him or his deep pockets."

"That temple is supposed to be one of the most magnetic places on the surface of the earth," Pavana said. "We've been trying for years to conduct research there. How'd this man get permission?"

The cell phone vibrated in Muni's palm.

Pavana took back the phone. "Huri News has another newsflash. Wow! Three major earthquakes and a tsunami have been reported around the globe."

Muni snatched back the cell phone and read. "A 7.3 in Jakarta, a 7.9 whopper in South America, and a 6.4 around Palo Alto, California. Plus, there was a devastating tsunami in the Galápagos Islands off the coast of Ecuador."

"What's going on?" Pavana wondered.

A smile spread across Muni's face. "Perhaps the Voices are preparing the way. Summon Faraw to watch Varya and follow me to the lab."

Faraw arrived ten minutes later, baby bag in tow. Muni and Pavana rushed back down the dirt path toward a small concrete building in the center of the Antakaale's estate. They called it the Command Center because the structure housed the various instruments that Muni, Pavana, and Gita—before she had attempted escape—used to measure Earth's magnetic field.

Muni glanced around, looking for anyone suspicious. Just last month they had caught a reporter from a magazine called *Science Sphere* snooping around the plantation. Somehow, she had sneaked through the gates and wanted to interview Muni. Members of the Antakaale quickly escorted the woman off the property, but it was a painful reminder that some people were still interested in the whereabouts of the former esteemed professor of geophysics, Benedykta Wójcik, PhD.

Pavana slipped a card into the security pad, the door popped open, and they stepped inside. A cool blast of air-conditioning greeted them.

"I'll prep the fluxgate magnetometer," Pavana said.

The fluxgate magnetometer was a sophisticated instrument no larger than a kitchen mixer that worked like a compass. Except, instead of a spinning needle, it used electromagnets to measure magnetic fields.

Muni sat down at a computer terminal. She logged onto the Geomagnetic Disturbance Lab's website based in Helsinki, Finland, to check various satellite readings that also measured the strength and direction of the magnetic field.

"Wow," Muni said, a hint of excitement in her voice. "Look at this."

"What is it?"

"According to data from the satellites, weak spots in the magnetic field are popping up everywhere in the Western Hemisphere. And the magnetic field is strengthening dramatically over the Indian Ocean."

Pavana looked over Muni's shoulder and pointed to a blue blip on the computer screen. "Whoa! Did you just see that? A major magnetic disturbance just happened at latitude longitude 34.8129° N, 111.8309° W."

"Where's that?" Muni wondered aloud as she googled the coordinates. "It's Red Rock State Park in Sedona, Arizona."

"What's going on?"

"You have your PhD from Imperial College London," Muni said, testing her. "You tell me."

Pavana thought for a moment. "Well, there's likely only one reason the field is weakening so dramatically," she explained. "The earth's magnetic poles are getting ready to flip."

"And why would flipping poles cause the field to weaken?"

"Because this is proven through analysis of seafloor magnetic anomalies. When a reversal of the magnetic poles happens, the shielding effect of Earth's magnetic field weakens, exposing the atmosphere to much higher levels of radiation."

Muni smiled. "Such a smart woman. You make the Voices so happy. Tell me the last verse of the *The Way to New Earth*."

"The Old Earth shall reverse from one end to the other," Pavana recited. "What was wrong shall be made right. The Voices will grant a New Earth for all those who hear."

"All the data suggests the magnetic north is moving toward Siberia," Muni said.

"Do you think the earthquakes and tsunami could have something to do with this?"

Muni sat up from the chair and paced the room. "Of

course, it does," she said. "But I also think it has something to do with that idiot *Doctor* Lennon Hatch and the explosion he caused at the temple."

"Huh?" Pavana asked, puzzled.

"If that powerful magnetic point on the globe was altered in some way, this may be the beginning of the cataclysmic shift the Voices whispered to me all those years ago. We'll need Gita's expertise in physical chemistry to ride this all the way. Prepare her for another indoctrination."

Pavana nodded dutifully and raced out the room.

Chapter Twelve
AXEL

Axel, Charu, and Megan walked quickly down the hall and maneuvered single file through a series of maze-like passageways. The place wasn't just a series of caves, but a beautiful underground shrine. Axel gazed in awe as several torches illuminated the place in a golden hue, but he was too consumed with thoughts of Daisha to truly appreciate the antiquity. The woody smell of sandalwood incense wafted in the still air. Large pillars carved with exquisite murals lined the perimeter of the space. Decorative tapestries of animals and Hindu gods hung from the ceiling. A depiction of a man with the head of an elephant captured Axel's attention.

"Who's that?" he whispered.

"Ganesha," Charu answered. "Yep. One of the most beloved Gods in all of Hinduism has the head of an elephant and body of a human."

"Very interesting," Axel said.

"You should read up on him. Good old Ganesha helps people remove obstacles. He also has an insatiable sweet tooth. Next time you see a statue of him, toss a candy bar at his feet and he'll bless you forever."

They came to a large opening covered with shimmering beads.

"This is Jag's chamber," Megan said.

A hand parted the beads, and a tall figured stepped into the dim light.

"Jag," Axel said. "Where's Larraj? We need to ask him something."

"I still can't find him," Jag said. "Kundan doesn't even know where he went."

"Then *you'll* have to help us," Megan said.

Jag raised his eyebrows. "Help with what?"

"We have a problem and thought there might be more to the palm leaf prophecy that could help us figure out what's happening."

Jag held up one finger, indicating for them to wait. He disappeared into his chamber and returned a moment later holding a manila envelope.

"I found this at the foot of my door this morning," Jag said. "It's addressed to Axel, and it's in Larraj's handwriting."

"What is it?" Axel asked.

Jag reached into the envelope and pulled out a single palm leaf. Axel remembered it looking just like the one Larraj had read to him back at the Sun Temple. The leaf was about the size and shape of a ruler. The faded squiggly lines of scrawled Sanskrit were barely legible.

"What's it say?" Megan asked.

"First things first," Jag said. "What is your problem?"

Megan explained about the earthquakes and tsunamis happening around the globe. How Axel's father and Daisha's mother were still studying the long-term effects of the X-Points and were unsure of what would happen when one was destroyed. She said the professors had instructed that if something went wrong, they'd need help in creating a new X-Point.

Jag stroked the day-old stubble on his chin. "And something indeed has gone wrong."

"We don't know what to do," Axel said. "Since you and Larraj were correct about the Sun Temple, maybe you can help us with this too."

"*We* do not help you," Jag said. "Larraj and I are just the keepers and interpreters of the palm leaves. The Seven Sages who wrote on them thousands of years ago get all the credit."

"Please, read me the leaf," Axel said. "It's addressed to me, after all."

Jag motioned them to come inside his chamber. Unlike the ornately decorated hallways, his room was plain. The only item of note besides a cot, dresser, and nightstand was a small altar with statues of various deities.

They sat on pillows in a semicircle while Jag carefully studied the palm leaf.

"A beam of light will pierce the Valley of the Moon and bring about a new day," Jag said, translating the Sanskrit to English. "There, the boy with hair the muddy color of the Narmada River and the girl, shadowy and beautiful like the goddess Parvati, will defeat the mother of daughters with two gems more powerful than the Syamantaka Jewels."

Axel's face lit up. "I'm the boy and Daisha is the girl!" he exclaimed. "If the prophecy says we have to go to this Valley of the Moon and defeat this mother of daughters, whoever that is, then Daisha must still be alive!"

"What are the two gems more powerful than the Syamantaka Jewels?" Charu asked.

"What are Syaman...taka Jewels, anyway?" Axel asked.

"The Syamantaka Jewels are said to have magical

powers," Jag explained. "They belonged to Surya, the Sun God. Whoever possessed them was divinely protected from natural disasters such as hurricanes, floods, earthquakes, or droughts."

"The two gems from the prophecy have to mean the two GeoPorts," Axel said. "What else could it be? We'll need both of them to defeat this so-called mother lady."

Megan nodded in agreement. "You're right about needing both GeoPorts and the fact that Daisha may still be alive. After what I've seen, I can't question the palm leaves."

Axel stood up. "Come on. We have to get out of these caves. I need to find Daisha."

"Let's go," Jag said, and he led them to another large room. Dappled bars of sunlight shined down on them through a partially concealed opening in the ceiling. A tall wooden ladder pointed toward the exit.

"Is your leg okay to climb?" Charu asked Axel.

Axel nodded. "It should be fine as long as I take it easy."

Jag was the first up followed by Charu, Axel, and Megan.

A warm, humid breeze greeted them as soon as they were outside. Jag quickly covered the opening with branches and stones to conceal the cave's location.

Axel took a deep breath. Fresh air mixed with flowery scents wafted in his nostrils. He had been in the caves for nearly a week and forgotten how much he missed the sunshine.

"I never want to go back down there again," Axel said.

"We shouldn't have to anymore," Jag offered, "unless it's by choice. From what I've heard, the Doctor and most of his men are now in Bhopal telling their side of the story to some very important state officials."

Axel scratched gently at his wound. "Where's Bhopal?"

"A city about forty-five kilometers from here," Charu answered.

"That means his men are probably too busy saving their own hides to look for us anymore," Megan said.

A group of Australian tourists strolled past, examining the ancient Stone Age art of the rock shelters. Axel had been underground so long he forgot this whole place was a UNESCO World Heritage Site.

"We need to find the location of this Valley of the Moon," Axel said.

Megan pulled out her iPhone and typed into Safari. "Ugh!" she groaned after reading the search results.

"What's wrong?" Charu asked.

"There are a ton of places known as the Valley of the Moon. Sonoma Valley in California, Ischigualasto Provincial Park in Argentina, Wadi Rum desert in Jordan, and even a Children's Fantasy Park in Tucson, Arizona. All of them are called the Valley of the Moon."

"Wow," Axel said a hint of amazement in his voice. "Daisha and I've been there."

"What do you mean *been there*?" Megan asked.

"The Children's Fantasy Park in Tucson. Our parents took us there the summer going into fifth grade. We also went to the Grand Canyon and the Four Corners Monument where Colorado, New Mexico, Utah, and Arizona meet."

"It could be a sign," Jag said. "Daisha may be in Arizona. I say that's where we look first."

"How do you propose we do that?" Axel asked. "We're in the middle of India, and my GeoPort won't take us there."

Axel's simple observation about their geographical location took the air out of everyone's enthusiasm. More tourists came and went as they meandered around the rock shelter, trying to figure how to get to Arizona. The only way to the United States was via a commercial airliner, which would be an extremely long flight plus layovers and long lines.

"How much is a one-way plane ticket from India to Arizona anyway?" Axel wondered.

"Could cost as much as two thousand dollars one-way," Megan answered.

"Two thousand dollars! Who has that kind of money?"

"Not me, I'm afraid," Charu said.

"That's just slightly higher than India's average per capita income," Jag added.

Axel slammed his flattened palm against a rock. "We have to figure out how to get there before something happens to her!"

An excited expression flashed on Megan's face. She reached into her satchel, rummaged around, and pulled out what looked like a credit card. She playfully waved the plastic under Axel's nose.

"Maybe we can use this," Megan said with a mischievous smile.

"Awesome!" Axel exclaimed. "Do you have enough credit to pay for all of us?"

"Yeah, right. My cards have been maxed out since I graduated from Stanford. But a young lady named Stiv might have a very large credit line."

Axel tilted his head, puzzled. "What in the world are you talking about? And who is Stiv?"

Megan handed Axel the card. It was a Visa for a person named Stiv Smith. Underneath the name were the words *Hatch Enterprises, LLC*. She then explained her whole undercover operation with the Doctor. How she had infiltrated his organization under a pseudonym and gained his trust, so much so that he had ordered his accountant to issue her a company credit card.

"But it can't be still active after all that happened at the Sun Temple," Axel said.

"He's right," Jag said. "Surely your card would have been canceled."

"There's only one way to find out," Megan said. She started tapping away on her phone. Five minutes later, they had their answer.

"Yes!" Megan squealed, pumping her fists. "The card still works! I've booked us four one-way tickets from Bhopal, India, to Tucson, Arizona."

Axel beamed. "Get ready, Daisha," he said. "I'm coming for you."

Chapter Thirteen

DAISHA

A piercing squawk from a soaring golden eagle jostled Daisha from her sleep. She opened her eyes to the brilliant crimson and orange of sunrise. All around her, giant red rocks jutted up into the sky. The scent of moist dirt and wild sage wafted in the air, and the sound of rushing water blasted in her ears.

Scenes from the previous day replayed in her mind. She remembered Warping with Loosha, landing at Red Rock State Park, the old couple, three college kids, park rangers riding horses, and hiding among the boulders near the stream.

21.52, 75.3, 78.14, 0.9786

The random numbers flashed in her mind. She took the GeoPort from her pocket and stared at the screen.

"What's going on with this thing?" Daisha wondered aloud. She looked at Loosha.

He was slumped against a boulder, eyes closed, head bobbing, a thin line of drool dripping out of his mouth.

Loosha opened his eyes. "Hun...a...whatta," he mumbled incoherently.

"You're dreaming," Daisha whispered. "Go back to sleep."

"What did you say, *dziewczyna*?" Loosha asked.

"You sure like that word."

"What word?"

"*Dziewczyna*. What does it mean anyway?"

Loosha yawned, stretched, and reoriented himself to the surroundings. He plucked out the pistol, checked to make sure it was loaded, and shoved it back into the holster. He then climbed a mound of rocks to look around.

"Girl," he said, peering down at her. "*Dziewczyna* means 'girl' in Polish."

Daisha sneered at him. "Coming from you, I assumed it meant something much more offensive. What's *boy* in Polish?"

"*Chłopak*."

"Then that's my new name for you."

Loud thumping sounds echoed on the trail above. Daisha recognized them instantly as horse hooves. Loosha scooted off the rocks and ordered Daisha back between the two boulders. Clouds of dust and dirt rained down on them as two park rangers galloped past.

"They're either on a random patrol or are looking for us," Daisha said.

Loosha climbed back on the rocks and peered down the trail. "Whatever the reason, they're gone," he said. "But I don't want to take any chances. We'll stay hidden for a while longer."

Pangs of hunger shot through Daisha's stomach. Her mouth was dry. She hadn't eaten or drank anything since yesterday afternoon. Every ounce of her being wanted to creep down to the stream and take a slurp, but she decided it wasn't a good idea. She had read a book back in sixth grade about a boy who was lost in the woods. The boy drank from a stream, caught a bug called *beaver fever*, and puked and pooped non-stop for a whole day.

"How long before we can Warp back to Palo Alto?" Loosha asked.

Daisha shrugged. "Not until the GeoPort starts beeping. What happens then is anyone's guess."

"I have money. Maybe we can wander out of this park and get some food."

They hiked down Apache Fire Trail, passing two groups of hikers. The park rangers on horseback were nowhere in sight. After resting at a scenic lookout, they hooked up with Coyote Ridge Trail. Forty-five minutes later, they came to Eagle's Nest, Smoke Trail, and finally to the Red Rock State Park's Miller Visitor Center. The parking lot was full of cars and RVs. Dozens of people meandered in and out of the stone buildings.

"There's a sign for the gift shop," Daisha said, pointing. "Maybe we can get something to drink and eat."

"Stick close to me," Loosha said, stuffing the pistol down his pants so not to draw attention. "If you see a park ranger looking at us suspiciously, prepare to run."

Daisha nodded and followed behind. Typical tourist items filled the gift shop. T-shirts, stuffed animals, magnets, key chains, hats, bumper stickers, books, maps, and a collection of high-end, handcrafted leather and woodcraft from local artisans. Loosha grabbed two matching Red Rock State Park baseball caps and backpacks. Daisha went straight for the snacks. She grabbed six bottles of water, several bags of chips, a couple handfuls of chocolate bars, and a bag of granola called Sagebrush Crunch.

The grand total was seventy-seven dollars and fifty-eight cents. Loosha pulled out a one-hundred-dollar bill from his wallet and handed it to the clerk, an older woman with thick gray hair piled high in a bun.

"Sorry, we can't accept bills over fifty dollars," the clerk said.

"But that's all I have," Loosha grumbled.

"Sorry, but it's policy."

Rage washed over Loosha's face. Daisha's heart dropped into her stomach as Loosha reached toward the pistol hiding in his waistband.

The deep voice of a man bellowed from behind them. "It's your lucky day, partner."

Daisha and Loosha turned and saw a park ranger, Smoky the Bear get-up and all, walking toward them.

"I can break your hundred with a fifty, two twenties, and a ten," the park ranger said.

Loosha stared at him blankly. Daisha took it upon herself to break the uncomfortable silence.

"Thank you," she said, yanking the one-hundred-dollar bill form Loosha's fingers and handing it the man. "I told my uncle to break it before we got here, but he was too excited to see the Red Rocks."

"Enjoy the park," the ranger said and left the gift shop.

Daisha finished paying for their items. The other customers looked on as both of them guzzled two bottles of water each and wolfed down a candy bar right on the spot. The water and sugar rush gave Daisha a needed boost of energy. They slipped on their caps, stuffed the backpacks with the rest of their stuff, and headed to the restroom.

From outside came a series of loud and astonished *oohs* and *ahhs*.

"What's that?" a woman's voice called out.

"The strangest rainbow I've ever seen," said a man.

"Alien invasion!" cried a boy.

Daisha and Loosha ran outside to see what the commotion was all about. What they saw nearly made their eyes pop out. Brilliant streaks of green, pink, yellow, red, and violet flashed across the blue morning sky. The colors danced and twirled like giant points of light pirouetting across the upper atmosphere.

"This is crazy," Loosha said, staring into the sky.

A man wearing a long-billed hat with a neck shield dropped to his knees in prayer, tears streaming down his cheeks. Several more people joined him as the heavenly light show became brighter and more fantastical.

"Mommy," a little brown-haired girl whimpered. "That thing's trying to eat the sun."

That was the exact moment when Daisha remembered what Megan had told her back at the Konanvlah Sun Temple in India.

"Scientists measure the sun in angles not latitude

and longitude," she said to herself, nearly reciting word for word Megan's mini-lecture back at the palm leaf library. "As in which direction and how high is the sun at any time of day. Solar declination, solar azimuth, solar elevation, and zenith angle. The only way to destroy the X-Point is to set the GeoPort directly toward the sun and meet the solar wind head on."

21.52, 75.3, 78.14, 0.9786

Daisha's knees buckled slightly as the source of the numbers came to her. "They're the ones Megan set on Axel's GeoPort!" she exclaimed. "This thing is still trying to send me to the sun! That's probably why the twenty-four-hour reset is out of whack and the time between Warps is getting shorter."

The GeoPort in Daisha's pocket vibrated to life. Loud beeping sounds rang in her ears. She plucked the unit from her pocket and saw the blue starbursts and same flashing numbers. Her excitement of a moment ago melted into fear. She felt her stomach clench as thoughts of why this was happening tumbled in her mind.

"The GeoPort's sending me to the sun, just like Megan said, but every time it does, a new X-Point opens up and it plops me back down to Earth," she said to herself. "What if next time it doesn't stop and I melt away like a modern day Icarus? The next time I Warp could be the last time."

Axel flashed in her mind—his kind, loving face draped in long brown locks. What if he was calling to her with his own GeoPort like some kind of solar wind walkie-talkie? He was out there somewhere, and she had to find him even if it meant risking her own life.

"Time to Warp, *chłopak*," Daisha said.

Loosha looked at the GeoPort. "Do those numbers mean Palo Alto?"

"No," Daisha said. "They're the way to Axel and Megan. I just know it. And you're going to help me find them."

Daisha grabbed Loosha's arm, pressed the SW button, and they both disappeared into the Warp.

Chapter Fourteen
MUNI

Muni sat in lotus position, eyes closed, head bobbing as the Voices swirled inside her brain.

"Guide me," she hushed softly. "Take us all to New Earth."

The Voices grew louder inside her skull. Chanting and humming like a symphony of angels. There were no commands or words of wisdom, only powerful images choreographed perfectly to match the spirit song. A vast, scorching desert flashed in her mind's eye. Thousands of swirling sand devils twisted and twirled among the barren dunes. Camels appeared carrying men in long white robes and keffiyeh headdresses. Her heart pumped wildly as two children entered the vision. Muni felt a sudden sense of dread. One was a black girl, the other a white boy. She saw their young faces clearly. They looked no older than thirteen or fourteen, but something about their essence was very ancient, powerful, and potentially dangerous to the Antakaale.

Muni followed them to a place of seven pillars of stone. This was the entranceway to New Earth. Muni reached out to the children, desperately trying to make them hear the Voices. Just as she was about to touch them, a scorching hot wind blew across her face. Pinpricks from the violently whipping sand stung her cheeks.

Her eyes snapped open. Sweat poured down her temples. Her breath came in quick huffs. She was no longer in the sizzling desert, but sitting in the breezy comfort of her open-air office. A tear rolled down her cheek. The Voices had given her many visions before, but none like this.

Verse seventy-two of the teachings burst from her throat.

"The final test will be with fire and heat," she uttered. "The dry Old Earth will give way to a moist New Earth. Do not fear the everlasting inferno, for it is only an illusion."

There was no mistaking what she had seen. Heat and fire directly relate to a hot desert. But where was this desolate place? Camels lived in North Africa, the

Middle East, and Central Asia. And who were these very strong children?

A knock came at her door.

Muni sat up from her pillows. "Yes," she said, her voice a little shaky from the vision.

"Gita's at the Command Center," Pavana's said through the door in her cheery British accent. "Re-indoctrination was a smashing success."

"Perfect. Give me a moment."

After composing herself, Muni put on a clean robe, slipped a lotus flower behind her ear, and walked down the dirt path toward the Command Center.

Gita was sitting at a computer terminal, a large bandage plastered across her forehead. She rubbed a hand across her newly cropped head. Pavana had shaved off her hair with a razor as a part of the cleansing and re-indoctrination ritual.

"I'm so happy you're back," Muni said. "The Soul Worms tried to get you, but the Voices vanquished them in glorious victory. Tell me verse twenty-seven of the teachings."

Gita stared at her. Her brown eyes and Muni's green eyes engaged in an intense game of who blinks first.

"The Voices are the only true voice," Gita said flatly. "Without them there is only silence."

Muni smiled, pleased to have won the game. Gita itched the bandage on her forehead.

"Don't worry about your battle scars," Pavana said. "They will heal, and our sacred symbol will shine bright upon you again."

"I just had an extremely lucid vision of verse seventy-two," Muni said.

"Do not fear the everlasting inferno for it is only an illusion," Pavana spouted.

"The Voices are communicating with me much more often now. The time to leave for New Earth is almost upon us."

"I want to see Cat—" Gita started to say but then corrected herself. "I mean, when can I see Varya?"

"After our work is done," Muni said. "Don't worry about her. She's safe in Faraw's care."

Gita's eyes narrowed, and her cheeks flushed with heat. "I want to see her. Now."

"You'll see her when I say so," Muni calmly replied. "Now, bring up the readings or you won't see her at all."

Gita opened her mouth to fire back but swallowed her words. She typed in her password and brought up the satellite readings of space weather. A split screen dedicated to phenomena like coronal mass projections, geomagnetic storms, solar radiation, sunspots, and the aurora appeared on the screen.

With a click of the mouse, Gita brought up the aurora forecast. Monitoring of the aurora was one of her daily duties. The aurora lights were the final cosmic process of the earth's complicated dance with the sun. They occurred when supercharged particles from the sun's atmosphere moved into Earth's atmosphere via the solar wind. According to Muni, the Voice's communicated directly to her through the solar wind. The stronger the phenomena, the closer they were to realizing New Earth.

A satellite image of the earth appeared on the screen. Normally, the swath of green representing the aurora hovered steadily over the northern hemisphere. But now that swath of green was on the move.

"This has to be a mistake," Gita blurted. "The aurora borealis doesn't just *move*."

"Unless there's a severe solar storm, which according to the analyses is *not* happening right now," Pavana added.

"The satellite readings are correct," Muni said. "The so-called northern lights have drifted as far south as Arizona in North America."

"Red Rocks State Park," Pavana said.

"Red Rocks what?" Gita wondered.

"Our flux magnetometer and satellite dish picked up a major magnetic disturbance yesterday," Muni explained. "That event happened at latitude 34.8129° N longitude 111.8309° W. Otherwise known as Red Rocks State Park in Sedona, Arizona. What do you think, Gita?"

Gita stood up and logged onto another computer.

"The only reason the aurora would be moving south is because Earth's magnetic field is weakening," Gita said.

"That's obvious," Pavana said. "But why is it happening now?"

Muni's penetrating green eyes glared at Pavana. "You already know what's going on," she said after a moment. "Or have you forgotten the last verse of the Voices teachings?"

"The Old Earth shall reverse from one end to the other," Pavana said with delight. "What was wrong shall be made right. The Voices will grant a New Earth for all those who hear."

A loud alert beep came from a computer terminal. The three of them gathered around and watched as a red, throbbing blip appeared above the continent of Africa.

"Wow," Pavana blurted. "There's been another major magnetic disturbance. This time it's at latitude 29.5347° N, longitude 35.4079° E."

Gita typed the coordinates into a Google search. "That's the Wadi Rum desert in Jordan," she said. "The place is stunning. Look at these photos."

Muni leaned in to Gita's computer monitor and nearly fell to the floor. The image was of a large mountain with seven rounded spires towering among the clouds. She took in a long, slow breath, her nerves tingling with excitement. Verse seventy-two and the vision of a hot desert tumbled in her mind.

"The Voices have shown me this place in my dreams!" Muni cried, her eyes wild with anticipation. "The magnetic disturbance in the desert! We've been waiting for the sign. The time has come to finally leave for New Earth."

Chapter Fifteen

AXEL

The road to Bhopal was bumpy, sweltering, and mildly nauseating. Axel sat with Charu and Megan in the back of a rickety pickup truck hauling stalks of sugar cane. Jag rode up front with the driver. Motorcycles and cars whizzed past them, churning up thick dust. The road hugged a muddy river on one side. Newer homes and bamboo shacks lined the other. Beyond was deep jungle broken up with fields of crops.

Farther in the distance, several skyscrapers jutted high into the sky.

"My parents live on the eighteenth floor of one of those tall buildings," Charu said.

"Which one?" Axel asked.

"Third one from the right." Charu turned to Megan. "How long is the flight to America?" she asked. "Can we stop in Hollywood? I want to stroll down the Walk of Fame."

Megan smirked at her. "It's a thirty-two-hour flight with four stops," she said. "Mumbai, London, Chicago, and Tucson."

Axel pinched off a woody piece of sugar cane and gave it a lick.

"Yuck!" he said, spitting it out. "I thought sugar cane would be sweet. This stuff tastes awful and reeks like an ashtray."

"The farmers burn the stalks to remove the outer leaves," Charu explained. "The chemicals released from the combustion are what creates the bad smell. Much processing has to happen to extract the sweetness."

Megan fanned the air in front of her nose. "Honey's my new sweetener of choice."

The mention of honey made Axel instantly think of Daisha. She used to buy bundles of honey sticks at the Downtown Palo Alto Farmers' Market. The girl sucked on those things like normal kids chewed bubble gum.

"What if we don't find her in Arizona?" Axel asked.

"There aren't that many places called Valley of the Moon," Megan said. "If she's not there, we go to the next place." She picked up her phone, opened a browser, and tapped the screen. "Major wow!" she exclaimed after a moment.

"What's wrong?" Jag asked, concerned.

"A newsflash about strange lights appearing over Arizona just popped up on my phone," Megan said. "Look at the pics."

Axel and Charu took turns looking at Megan's phone.

"Are they the aurora borealis?" Charu asked.

"Looks like it," Axel said. "I've seen them before. When I was nine, some university in Iceland invited my dad to speak, and I went with him."

Charu handed Megan back the phone. "That can't be possible," she said.

"Well, if it's not the borealis then the world's coming to an end," Megan said.

Charu giggled. "Highly unlikely."

"I'm checking out the GMDL website," Megan said. "That stands for the Geomagnetic Disturbance Lab based at Helsinki University in Finland. If anything wacky is going in the upper atmosphere, they'll report it."

The truck veered left and right, attempting unsuccessfully to avoid the many potholes. Axel, Megan, and Charu held on tight as the truck realigned its wheels and continued down the road.

"Everyone okay back there?" Jag shouted from the passenger's side window.

Megan gave him a thumbs-up. "Looks like we have another major geomagnetic disturbance," she said.

"Where is it?" Axel asked.

"It says the disturbance happened at latitude 29.5347° N, longitude 35.4079° E," Megan said. "Let me switch over to latilongi.com and find the global position."

Before Megan had a chance to look up the coordinates, the pickup lurched hard off the road. Axel's stomach leaped into his throat. He thought they were avoiding another pothole, but he saw the earth trembling violently beneath them. A large house to their right slipped off its foundation and crumpled to the ground. Panicked screams echoed from the rubble. A series of loud explosions blasted in the distance. Plumes of black smoke rose above the Bhopal skyline. A large fissure in the earth formed on the road just ahead of them. The driver hit the brakes, but it was too late. The pickup skidded sideways and fell directly into the crevice.

The truck slammed to a stop. Jag and the driver thumped headfirst into the windshield. Sugar cane stalks flew all around as Axel, Megan, and Charu hung on to the truck bed's sidewalls for dear life.

There was another series of violent tremors, and then everything fell silent.

"We were in an earthquake," Megan said, gasping for air.

"Ahhh," Jag groaned from up front.

"Are you okay?" Megan hollered.

Jag didn't answer. Axel watched as he crawled out the truck's window and climbed from the crevice. Blood dripped down his face. After a moment, the driver came out of the other side and scuttled to safety. Fortunately, they hadn't fallen too far.

"Are any of you hurt?" Jag asked.

Everyone shook their heads.

"Then give me your hand," Jag said as he reached for Charu.

He pulled her up and did the same for Megan and Axel. Several people crawled from the rubble of the destroyed house. They looked to be in shock, but no one appeared hurt.

The truck driver knelt on the side of the road, head in his hands. "My haul is ruined," he moaned. "I've lost a lot of money."

"At least you didn't lose your life," Jag said, trying to cheer him up.

"I've been in a few California quakes before," Megan said. "But nothing like this. This had to be a 7.0 or higher."

Tears streamed down Charu's face. She was looking at the destruction ahead. "My parents and brother live in Bhopal."

Axel put his arm around her. "It's okay," he said gently.

"What about Kundan back in the caves?" Megan asked.

Jag took off his shirt and dabbed at the cut on his forehead. "The epicenter appears to be directly in Bhopal," he said quietly. "The Rock Shelters are far enough away."

They all sat there for several minutes, soaking in what had just happened to them and not quite believing it at the same time. A small girl from an intact house nearby brought them three unopened bottles of Mulshi spring water. Axel, Megan, and Charu shared two bottles, leaving Jag and the driver to split the other one.

"What do we do now?" Megan asked.

"Obviously, we can no longer go to Bhopal," Jag said. "Let's start walking back to the caves. Hopefully, we can catch a ride from someone."

They thanked the family for the water and started walking. Dozens of destroyed homes, toppled trees, and wrecked cars lined the road. Several people scurried around the ruins. Sirens blared in the direction of Bhopal.

An old man with long white hair and only one leg sat on the side of the road.

"*Om tryambakam yajamahe sugandhim pushti wardhanam*," he repeated in a singsong voice.

"What's he saying?" Axel asked Charu.

"He's chanting a mantra for healing," she answered.

A sudden urge to cry came over Axel. Tears formed at the corners of his eyes. Charu hugged him tight. His own heart needed healing, because the thought of never seeing Daisha again was unbearable.

Chapter Sixteen
DAISHA

A clump of dry sand clogged Daisha's mouth. She sat up, spit out the grit, and looked around. There was nothing but a dry, barren desert as far as the eye could see. Loosha was beside her on his hands and knees dry heaving from plunging into the Warp.

"Where are we?" Loosha asked, wiping sand from his eyes.

"Mars," Daisha said, and she was only half joking.

Giant rock outcrops poked from the desert floor. Wind whipped through the harsh landscape. The heat was so scorching and intense, she couldn't even tell what time of day it was.

Loosha stood up. "Looks like we're still in Arizona," he said.

Daisha's heart sunk. She had hoped the GeoPort would have dropped her back in India with Axel. But it looked like she was still in the United States with Loosha by her side, probably only a hundred miles or so from Red Rocks State Park.

She looked at her GeoPort.

The unit flashed with the numbers 21.52, 75.3, 78.14, 0.9786, same as before.

"We have to get out of this heat," Loosha said. "The temperature feels like it's well over a hundred degrees."

Daisha rolled her eyes. "And silly me forgot to pack my shades, bikini, and sunblock. Let's head back to Palo Alto so I can get them."

"You're very funny," Loosha said with a chuckle. "Looks like there might be some shade in those narrow gorges between the rocks."

Their destination was a lot farther away than they thought. They hiked single file through the red sand, sweat pouring down their faces, backpacks bobbing on their shoulders. A waft of Loosha's sweat and body odor made Daisha's nose crinkle. Neither of them had showered for days. After an hour tramp and exhausting climb over two very high sand dunes, they came to a series of large rock ridges.

The shade provided instant relief from the direct sun. They crouched in the sand, wiping off sweat and going through the contents of their backpacks. They had two bottles of water each plus several bags of chips, chocolate bars, and Sagebrush Crunch.

Daisha twisted open a bottle of water and started chugging. After four gulps, Loosha swiped the bottle away.

"Give me that back!" Daisha snapped.

"You've had enough," Loosha retorted. "We need to conserve our resources. Who knows how long we'll have to survive out here."

Loosha was right, but Daisha wasn't going to give him the satisfaction of knowing it. She snapped off a hunk of chocolate and plopped it in her mouth. "May I have some chocolate at least?" she said sarcastically.

"Half a bar," Loosha said. "No more. Didn't you see that movie *Alive* about the soccer players stranded in the Andes? I don't want to eat you when we run out of food."

Daisha gave Loosha a disgusted grimace and zipped up her backpack. The sun was growing higher in the sky. The heat was so intense that even the rock shade had lost its comfort.

"Let's go deeper into the gorge," Daisha suggested. "It may be cooler."

Loosha nodded, and they moved farther into the rock formations. Relief from the scolding sun was immediate. Ancient petroglyphs appeared scrawled into the rock. The drawings were of humans and animals. Some of the people were holding bows and arrows. The animals looked like horses and goats with long horns. Other images were of symbols like lines and circles.

"We're totally near the Grand Canyon," Daisha said. "These look exactly like the petroglyphs we studied in school during a unit on ancient people of the southwest."

Drip, drip, drip.

Daisha's ears perked. "Do you hear that?"

Loosha cocked his head, listening carefully. "No. What do you hear?"

They trudged deeper into the gorge. Broken shafts of light came from above. The *drip, drip, drip* noise grew louder. After a few more yards, Daisha discovered the source of the sound.

"Look!" she exclaimed.

Water dribbled from the rocks above and sloshed into a small pool below. Daisha kneeled down and splashed her face and neck with the cool water. Loosha did the same.

"I never thought I'd be so happy to see a stagnant puddle of water," Daisha said.

Loosha took off his shirt, dipped it in the water, and wiped under his armpits. "Out here in the desert even the smallest amount of water is precious," he said.

"What do we do now?"

"We'll stay here until dark. It will be much cooler at night, and we can walk to the nearest town. Considering we're in Arizona, one shouldn't be too hard to find."

For the next several hours, they sat at the pool, sharing a bag of chips and sipping from their plastic water bottles. A million thoughts ran through Daisha's head, mostly about her old life—and Axel's—back in Palo Alto. When Loosha dozed off, she took the opportunity to ease the GeoPort from her pocket. If another set of coordinates were flashing on the screen, she was going to Warp there *without* him.

Her hopes deflated like a four-day-old party balloon. They were the same numbers that had gotten her here. For no reason other than boredom, she found a hunk of rock on the ground and etched the coordinates along with her name on the rock wall.

21.52, 75.3, 78.14, 0.9786

DAISHA

Before she could scribble the date, a series of loud crunching sounds caught her attention. She quickly bolted upright and nudged Loosha.

"Wha...huh," he mumbled groggily.

"Do you hear that? It sounds like footsteps."

Loosha stood up and yanked the pistol from its holster. "I hear it," he whispered. "Get behind me."

Daisha did as she was told. The footsteps grew louder—*clomp, clomp, clomp*—echoing off the rock walls.

Loosha held up his pistol and aimed down the gorge. A long shadow appeared on the rocks. Daisha was shaking. The shadow grew larger until its source finally stepped into the light.

"It's—it's—" Loosha stuttered.

"A camel!" Daisha cried.

Chapter Seventeen
GITA

Gita sat at her computer, monitoring three violent, unprecedented volcanic eruptions, all of which had occurred within the last twenty-four hours. One was Redoubt Volcano, Alaska. The other took place at Kilauea Volcano, Hawaii. The most devastating occurred at Mount Hood Volcano, Oregon.

"Mount Hood Volcano hasn't been active in over two hundred years," she said with disbelief.

"Do not fear the everlasting inferno for it is only an illusion," Pavana said, reciting from *The Way to New Earth*. "The Voices will guide and protect us."

Gita thought of her mother who lived in Portland, Oregon. The last time she had spoken with her was over two years ago right before joining the Antakaale. She had been fourteen weeks pregnant with Catalina. Her mother had been so excited to find out she was going to be a grandmother. The impulse to pick up a phone and check on her was overwhelming, but she knew that would not happen.

"Another one!" Pavana screeched.

"What is it?" Gita wondered.

"They've just reported a tsunami in Pakistan along the Makran Coast. Hundreds are presumed dead."

Gita shook her head in disgust at Pavana's excitement over the loss of life. A tear rolled down her cheek. Not for the tsunami and volcano victims, but for her daughter. Muni still hadn't allowed her to see Catalina, and her heart was breaking.

"Play it cool," she whispered under her breath and wiped the tear away.

"Sorry?" Pavana asked. "Did you say something?"

"No, I just..." Gita started to say when a breaking news ticker flashed across the screen: *Mass Deaths of Thousands of Birds Reported around the Globe.*

She clicked the link, thinking the events had something to do with the tsunamis, volcanoes, and earthquakes. But to her astonishment, the deaths were nowhere near any of the plate tectonic disasters. According to reports, beachgoers had found thousands of migratory great cormorants dead along the coast of the United Arab Emirates. Also found dead were hundreds of thousands of Canada geese in and around Seneca Falls, New York, and an account of several thousand dead hummingbirds from Sky Islands, Arizona.

"Birds are dying all over the world," Gita said.

"How is that possible?" Pavana questioned.

Gita showed her the reports.

"Remarkable," Pavana muttered, eyes wide as she read.

For a flickering moment, Gita saw Pavana's inner scientist come to the surface and the outer Antakaale fade into the background. She took advantage of the situation, attempting to pry open the tiny crack in Pavana's armor.

"I can't help but think of the Triassic-Jurassic period," Gita said.

Pavana nodded. "When some eighty percent of Earth's species went extinct. Are you thinking what I'm thinking?"

"If it's about dropping oxygen levels then we're on the same page. When that reversal of the magnetic poles happened over two million years ago, it caused a major dip in Earth's breathable atmospheric air."

"This could be the proverbial canary in the coal mine."

Gita's heart skipped with excitement. They were talking like two geophysics professors, not devout followers of a fanatic who preached the end of the world.

"I wish we were back in my lab at UC Berkeley," Gita said.

Pavana gave her a puzzled glance.

"I mean, we would have access to all of the equipment needed to probe into this full bore," Gita clarified. "Where was your professorship again?"

"I...um," Pavana stuttered, like she was trying to retrieve a long-lost memory. "It was...uh...the University of Bristol."

Gita smiled. "I've been there. It's such a beautiful city with the Clifton Suspension Bridge, Cheddar Gorge, Bristol Cathedral. Were you born there?"

"Verse twenty-nine...hearing the Voices for the first time is like being reborn into—"

"Do you have any brothers or sisters?" Gita interrupted, desperately trying to keep Pavana from accessing Muni's teachings.

Pavana's face grew pale, like she was suffering the first sharp pangs of stomach flu. She collapsed into a chair. Sweat poured down her temples, and her breathing became labored.

"What's your real name?" Gita asked. "Do you miss your mother?"

"The Voices are like oxygen," Pavana mumbled under her breath. "You cannot see them, but need them to..."

Gita jumped out of her chair and cradled Pavana's face gently between her palms. "Please," she pleaded. "Take me to Cat...Varya. We can leave here. Go back to our old lives. Our families desperately miss us. The Voices aren't real. Muni doesn't..."

Pavana's hand reared back and slapped Gita hard across the face. Gita stumbled backward, her cheek and the wound on her forehead stinging with pain. They wrestled on the floor. Chairs overturned, drinking glasses shattered, a laptop crashed to the ground.

"The Voices speak the truth!" Pavana cried, pinning Gita to the ground.

"Have you ever heard the Voices yourself?" Gita spit back.

"Muni is the dreamer, the listener, the interpreter."

"That woman's a crazy old witch! She just hears voices in her head!"

The door to the Command Center flew open.

"Muni!" Pavana gasped.

Their leader gripped both girls by the backs of their

gowns and forcibly pried them apart.

"Soul Worms!" Muni yelled at the top of her lungs. "The Voices order you to leave these girls! Verse fifty-three says that all anger, argument, resentment, and lies be cast away so the Voices may enter all who believe!"

"But Gita said—" Pavana panted.

"Silence!" Muni roared. "Compassion is our gift. Gita has been attacked by the Soul Worms. If they gain entry once, they will try again and again. You should know this."

Gita was on her hands and knees, crying deep guttural wails that reverberated around the concrete room.

"Sob, my dear daughter," Muni said. "The Voices teach us that tears are great purifiers. Tell me verse forty-one."

"Give your pain to the Voices," Gita said in a barely audible whisper.

"Louder!" Muni cried and gripped the back of Gita's neck.

Tears streamed down Gita's face. She felt utterly helpless to the woman now towering over her. Muni had taken her child away, and now she held sway over her very life and death.

Muni bent down and whispered into Gita's ear. "Death comes to those who no longer hear the Voices.

Think of Varya. Do you want her to think Faraw is her mother? Tell me verse forty-one. Now."

"Give your pain to the Voices!" Gita bawled. "And the Voices will give you life and never leave you."

Muni's released her grip from Gita's neck. She ran a hand through her long silver hair and readjusted the lotus flower behind her ear.

"Follow me to the Temple," she instructed. "I've assembled everyone. It's time to tell the good news. We'll be leaving shortly for New Earth."

Chapter Eighteen

AXEL

Megan googled the location of the new coordinates on her phone.

29.5347° N, 35.4079° E

"Where is it?" Axel asked, barely able to contain his excitement.

"No service," Megan said after a moment. "The quake must've knocked out the cell tower."

Axel tossed up his hands in exasperation. "Ugh! We have to know where those latitude and longitude numbers are coming from. I need to find Daisha!"

"Nothing can be done about it now," Jag said. "We need to help these people whose homes have been destroyed by the tremors." He turned to Charu. "As soon as cell service is back up, we'll check on your family. I'm sure they're okay."

For the next several hours, Axel, Charu, Megan, and

Jag helped search for missing people and animals. When they had accounted for everyone in the immediate area, it was time to clear rubble from the road so emergency vehicles could pass. Megan and Charu filled wheelbarrows and wagons. Jag and Axel took up shovels and loaded debris into the backs of pickup trucks that had miraculously survived the disaster. Oddly enough, the only homes left standing were the bamboo shacks. All of the newer homes made of concrete and steel had crumpled like Jenga blocks.

29.5347° N, 35.4079° E

The new coordinates flashed in Axel's mind with every shovelful of wreckage he dumped into the truck beds. He was convinced Daisha was on the other end of those numbers. She had to be. If only his unit worked properly. He'd press the SW button and Warp right next to her.

An older woman with tear tracks on her dusty face brought them plates of jasmine rice, boiled vegetables, and naan. After eating, they went back to work until most of the road was clear. A steady stream of emergency vehicles like ambulances, fire trucks, and police cars followed.

"Maybe we can catch a ride with a car leaving from Bhopal," Jag suggested.

"How far are the caves?" Megan asked.

"Over thirty kilometers," Charu answered. "Without a ride, it's a good six- or seven-hour walk."

"I don't think I'm up for that kind of hike after all this work," Axel said. "What should we do?"

"Let's just stay here for the night and rest," Jag suggested. "Tomorrow, we should be able to catch a ride to the rock shelter."

When the work was over for the day, a somber, depressing mood settled over the area. Nearly everything was gone. The earthquake had destroyed houses, animal huts, religious shrines, schools, roadside restaurants and markets, and even much of the surrounding crops.

People crowded around fires when evening fell, more for camaraderie and comfort than warmth. Axel, Jag, Megan, and Charu sat around their own blaze. Jag chucked in scraps of wood and scrounged tree branches to keep the flames going.

"Oooh!" Megan chirped. "I'm getting a bar on my phone."

"They must be getting the cell towers working," Jag said.

Axel peeked over Megan's shoulder. "Google the coordinates," he said.

"What are they again?" Megan asked.

"29.5347° N, 35.4079° E," Axel answered.

Megan typed in the numbers. They watched as the search engine sputtered, stopped, and sputtered some more. The phone was trying its hardest, but the signal wasn't strong enough.

"One bar is a good sign," Charu said. "That means Vodafone is working hard to get the transmission up and running again."

Axel stood up and stretched. "I need to go for a walk," he said and stepped away from the fire.

"Wait for me," Charu said, running to catch up to him.

They walked down the road together. A cow approached them. Axel patted its head and the bovine moved on.

"Do people in India really worship cows?" Axel asked.

Charu giggled. "What do you mean?"

"I heard cows in India are revered. You can't kill them or eat their meat."

"No, Hindus do not worship cows, but they are held in high esteem. They're free to roam wherever they desire."

"If you came to America, your head would explode at the way we treat cows and other livestock. It's pretty disgusting."

Charu smiled gently at him, and they continued walking. A million stars shined high and bright in the sky. Axel picked out the Big and Little Dippers. He soon saw Gemini, the Twins; Taurus, the Bull; and Orion, the Hunter.

"I see you enjoy gazing at the stars," Charu said.

"Yes. Daisha and I used to hunt for constellations back in Palo Alto."

"Is Daisha your girlfriend?"

Axel paused, not quite knowing how to answer. "No," he said after giving his response some thought. "We're more like brother and sister. I've known her my whole life. We don't have anyone but each other as far as family goes."

"In India, we call constellations *nakshatras*. I've studied the sky a lot."

"Oh, yeah? Have you ever heard of Pisces? Daisha and I've been trying to find that constellation since we were little kids."

"You mean Revati," Charu said. "That's the Hindu name for the star on the edge of the Pisces constellation."

Axel looked at her with raised eyebrows. "Wow. You really know your astrology."

"Astronomy, not astrology. I just love the science of

the stars and their connection to our world." Charu pointed into the sky. "There it is. Do you see it?"

Axel looked up, squinting his eyes. He scanned the sky for the Great Square of Pegasus. Pisces was directly below, along with Aquarius. At least that's what he had read. He had never actually found the constellation while lying in his backyard.

"I'll show you," Charu said.

She took hold of Axel's hand and raised it into the sky along with hers. As their fingers intertwined, she traced Pisces, a long V-shape across the sky. All of the constellation's major stars came into focus: Eta, Gamma, Omega, Iota, Omicron, and Alpha.

"Amazing," Axel said, a hint of awe in his voice. "I've never seen Pisces like that."

Axel lowered his hand, fingers still tightly tangled with hers. He didn't let go and neither did she. A strange yet pleasant fluttering sensation tingled in his stomach. They continued walking hand-in-hand down the road. Dozens of fires broke up the darkness. Both of them were extremely thankful that no one in the surrounding countryside had lost their lives.

When they were about to turn around and go back to Jag and Megan, a loud chirping sound rang in their ears. The GeoPort in Axel's front pocket vibrated to life.

"What's that noise?" Charu asked.

Axel let go of her hand, reached into his pocket, and pulled out the GeoPort.

"It's my GeoPort!" he exclaimed. "It's working again!"

"Why would it be working now?" Charu asked. "There was just an earthquake and cell phones aren't even working."

"GeoPorts don't work like cell phones," Axel said. He paused, trying to remember how exactly the devices *did* work. "Satellites capture electrons in the solar wind. They then channel that energy through the X-Point and to our GeoPorts...Well, that's how it worked before we got rid of the X-Point. Now I don't really know what's going on."

"It sounds like the way a cell phone works," Charu said. "Except instead of cellular towers sending the signal, the GeoPort uses satellites. What if being underground in the rock shelters made it so the GeoPort didn't get the signal?"

"Wow, I hadn't thought of it like that," Axel said, blushing. "My GeoPort wasn't broken—I just needed to plug it in!"

"What does that SW button mean?" Charu asked.

"It means Satellite Warp. If my unit's really working properly, all I have to do is type in coordinates, press the button, and I'd fly through the Warp to that very spot on the planet."

"Some place like 29.5347° N, 35.4079° E?"

Axel smiled at her and typed in the mystery coordinates. The latitude and longitude numbers shined neon green. Blue starbursts illuminated the unit's casing.

"We better go back and show this to Megan," Charu suggested.

Charu reached out and took Axel's hand again just as he pressed the SW button. Both of them exploded into puffs of smoke and electrical discharge.

Chapter Nineteen
DAISHA

The camel barely gave them a glance as it headed straight for the stagnant pool of water. The massive creature lowered its long neck and started drinking. Loud slurps from its thick tongue echoed off the rock walls of the gorge. When it was full, the camel lifted its head and stared directly at Daisha and Loosha.

"Do camels bite?" Daisha asked.

Loosha shrugged. "Don't know."

Daisha looked closer and saw a large white spot on its hump. There was a leather harness around its head along with a cloth saddle draped across its back.

"This camel must belong to someone," she said.

"Get out of here!" Loosha hollered, trying to shoo the animal away.

The camel looked at Loosha with its huge brown eyes and sprayed a wad of sticky white froth right in his face.

Daisha howled with laughter.

"Ahhh!" Loosha cried with disgust, wiping away the saliva. "I'll shoot that mangy creature!"

"You will do no such thing," Daisha said and stood between Loosha and the camel.

A voice called out.

"Jamel! Jamel!"

Daisha and Loosha shot each other an anxious glance.

"Jamel! Come!" the voice shouted again, this time getting closer.

Loosha cocked his pistol. Daisha scooted behind him for protection. Shuffling footsteps grew louder until finally a boy of ten or eleven appeared from the shadows. He had big dark eyes and donned a long white robe with a red-and-white checkered keffiyeh covering his head.

A stunned look came over the boy's face when he saw Daisha and Loosha standing against the rocks. He grabbed the camel's lead and tugged the animal away from the water.

"Who...are...you?" the boy asked, struggling to translate into English. "Did you...separate from...tour group?"

"Where are we?" Loosha barked.

"Uh...um," the boy stuttered, obviously afraid of Loosha's intimidating presence.

"You're right," Daisha interjected. "We got separated from our tour group. Can you help us?"

The boy smiled. "Yes. Come with me."

Daisha and Loosha followed the boy and camel out of the gorge. Goose bumps popped out on Daisha's skin when she hit the open desert. A brilliant orange sun was setting on the horizon. The temperature had dropped dramatically. She wondered how a place so blistering hot during the day could get so uncomfortably cold as evening grew nearer.

"Where are we?" Loosha asked again as they followed the boy and camel through the sand.

"Wadi Rum Protected Area," the boy said. "Camp is not far from here. Our family tour is authentic desert experience. Not near other tourist camps."

"What's he talking about?" Loosha asked.

Daisha shrugged. The boy was dressed in Arabic garb. That and the fact there was a camel traveling with them could only mean they were in the Middle East or perhaps North Africa. Their theory of still being in Arizona was several thousand miles off.

"What country is this?" Daisha asked.

The boy looked at her with an amused expression. "Jordan," he said. "Where else would you be?"

"There's your answer," Daisha said to Loosha. "We're in the Middle Eastern desert."

After twenty minutes of trekking, they came to a series of rocky outcrops. The boy let go of the camel's lead, allowing the animal to romp away toward a caravan of other camels roaming freely among the scrub.

"You're going to lose that camel again," Daisha said.

"Our camels do as they wish," the boy said. "Only that one roams far from us."

"What's your name?"

"Yaseen," the boy said. "And what are your names?"

"I'm Daisha. Mr. Grumpy Face is called Loosha."

Loosha frowned at her. "I'm not in the mood, *dziewczyna*."

They followed the boy through a passageway among the rocks. Daisha heard the sound of an acoustic guitar, laughter, and singing. What she saw next nearly blew her mind. They were inside a small, natural amphitheater among the boulders. Three colorful tents, two Toyota SUVs, and one large cargo van sat among the rocks. A man dressed like Yaseen tended an outdoor oven. The spicy smell of delicious food wafted in the air, making Daisha's stomach grumble with hunger.

"I'm starving for real food," she said. "I've only eaten potato chips and candy bars for nearly two days."

"*Taeam* will be ready soon," Yaseen said. "Wait here. I will get my uncle."

The sun had now completely disappeared over the horizon. Daisha shivered in the cool air and looked into the sky. Stars filled the beautiful night sky. Never in her life did the darkness seem so vivid and alive. Shooting stars rocketed across the cosmos before disappearing into oblivion. The constellations were so close it was like she could almost reach up and yank a handful from the sky.

Yaseen and a tall man emerged from the largest tent. The man was dressed in traditional Arab clothing. He was bigger than Loosha, but much friendlier looking.

"*Ahlan wa sahlan*," the man said with a smile. He handed Daisha and Loosha each a bottle of water.

"Thanks," Daisha said, twisting off the cap and taking a big slurp.

"My name is Khaled. Do you have a reservation with us? Because we're currently booked for the next month."

"We were separated from our tour group," Daisha said.

"We need help getting back to a town or city," Loosha added.

"What city did you fly into?" Khaled asked.

"I...uh," Loosha stammered.

"King Hussein International in Aqaba?" Khaled pressed. "Or perhaps Queen Alia International up in Amman?"

"King Hussein," Daisha blurted.

Khaled nodded. "Aqaba isn't far. Tomorrow morning someone can take you back to the Wadi Rum Visitor Center. There you can catch a bus to Aqaba. You will need to pay for the *ghaz*."

"I have plenty of money," Loosha said.

"Very good," Khaled uttered a few sentences to Yaseen in Arabic, and the boy ran off. "Yaseen will bring you blankets. All of our tents are full with guests, but you can sleep here next to the fire. We will bring you food."

After a satisfying dinner of rice, lamb, pita, and lentils, Daisha and Loosha climbed under their blankets next to the roaring fire. The temperature had dropped so low Daisha could see her breath. A smile spread across her face when she saw the Big and Little Dippers stretched across the night sky. She and Axel used to lie in the grass at night back in Palo Alto, trying to name all the constellations. It hadn't been easy because of the city lights, but they had managed to pick out a few like the two Dippers. Others were Gemini, the Twins; Taurus, the Bull; and Orion, the Hunter. However, locating Pisces had been nearly impossible, mostly because the stars in the constellation were dim.

But way out here in the middle of the vast Jordanian desert, Daisha saw Pisces as clear as day. She used her finger to trace its long V-shape against the sparkly backdrop of the night sky.

"Can you see it, Axel?" she whispered. "When we meet again, I'll show you how to find it."

She yawned, her eyelids fluttered, and she fell fast asleep.

Chapter Twenty

MUNI

The Antakaale's chartered private jet from Negombo, Sri Lanka, to Aqaba, Jordan, had cost more than two hundred thousand dollars. The flight was one way with first-class amenities for all. Money was not an issue. Thanks to several of Muni's wealthy devotees, she had a financial portfolio worth twenty million dollars, not counting pricey real estate like the tea plantation, a Central Park West New York City apartment, and a Malibu oceanfront home. She had yet to tell them why they were flying to the Middle East, and no one questioned her motives.

Two JETT tour buses and one rented SUV with tinted windows were waiting for them when they landed. The followers and the children hopped onto the buses. Muni, Gita, and Pavana slipped into the SUV. She handed the chauffeur a wad of cash, and they headed for a place called the Wadi Rum Visitor Center.

"We have plenty of work to do before transitioning to New Earth," Muni said, opening her laptop. The chauffeur didn't speak a word of English, so she wasn't concerned about him eavesdropping.

Pavana and Gita opened their laptops. Gita no longer wore a bandage on her forehead. Her scratches had nearly healed, and the Antakaale's sign once again shined brightly upon her.

"Be grateful for the Voices," Gita recited. "They are love, and their truth is for all who hear."

"Verse sixteen, one of my favorites," Muni said with a smile. "I still remember where I was when they whispered that into my ear."

"Where were you?" Pavana asked.

"I was still living in my little bungalow on North Michigan Avenue in Pasadena," Muni said. "The same day I officially resigned my professorship at Caltech."

"Praise the Voices," Gita spouted with enthusiasm. "They are the only truth, the only utterance worth hearing. Verse seventeen of *The Way to New Earth*."

Muni cupped Gita's hands in her own. "Your brief daily visits with Varya are keeping you in good spirits," she said. "You, me, and the little one will pass through the gates of New Earth together."

Gita nodded and typed into her computer. Pavana did the same. The Voices not only communicated to Muni in spiritual verses but also with science—advanced subjects like geophysics, chemistry, calculus, biology, and even economics.

"According to the data, the Wadi Rum desert is experiencing major geomagnetic disturbances," Pavana said.

Gita peeked at Pavana's computer screen. "Very similar to the instabilities around the Konanavlah Sun Temple at the time of the explosion."

"This place is the entryway to New Earth," Muni said. "The Voices gave me the vision of a vast, scorching desert, swirling sand devils, seven pillars, men in Arab dress, and the two children."

"Who were the children?" Pavana asked. "Were they ours?"

Muni shook her head. "They were older. Young teenagers. One was a striking black girl. The other was a white boy with long, flowing brown hair."

"Obviously *he* wasn't one of us," Gita said. "What did they have to do with your vision?"

Muni stared out the window. The Aqaba suburbs were turning into countryside. A flat, featureless desert stretched as far as the eye could see. A shudder wiggled up her spine. The two children of the vision had frightened her. They seemed ancient and powerful. Muni remembered reaching out to the kids, desperately trying to make them hear the Voices. But they had refused to listen to her.

Climb atop the Seven Pillars of Wisdom, where New Earth awaits. Two in youth will guide you, but they will not hear the Voices. Only one of you will survive.

This was the final verse of *The Way to New Earth.* However, Muni did not include it in the book. The other Antakaale had never heard the words before. Not even trusted confidants like Pavana. The prophecy was too confusing and cryptic. She did not want to frighten her followers and cast doubt in their minds.

"Three more events!" Pavana screeched.

"What are you talking about?" Muni asked.

"I just got a news flash on my phone. A massive 8.6 earthquake just happened in Bhopal, India. The quake destroyed much of the city and immediate rural areas."

"And the other two?" Gita wondered.

"There's been another devastating tsunami in the Pacific," Pavana continued. "Just like the Galápagos Islands. Viti Levu, the main island that makes up Fiji, is now completely submerged. And finally, the so-called supervolcano under Yellowstone National Park in the

United States is acting up for the first time in seventy thousand years. Hundreds of thousands of people in Wyoming, Montana, and Idaho have been evacuated."

"Never in recorded history have so many natural disasters happened within days of each other," Gita said.

"Bring up the satellite readings," Muni ordered.

Gita typed into the computer. "The aurora borealis can now be seen as far south as Ecuador," she said. "And Earth's magnetosphere is weakening in several locations. Radiation may be leaking into our atmosphere at unprecedented levels."

"Electron diffusion region," Muni muttered.

Pavana raised her eyebrows. "Excuse me?"

"It's another name for an X-Point," Gita explained. "They're places where Earth's magnetic field and the Sun's magnetic field meet. I remember a couple Stanford professors were conducting research on the subject. Professors Jack and Tandala."

The car slowed down and swerved slightly. They looked out the windows and saw that several large rocks had rolled into the road. The chauffeur looked into the back seat and waved his hand, indicating everything was okay.

"I've been out of academia for a long time," Muni said. "But the Voices still command me to keep up with all the new research. Those two Stanford professors you mentioned were funded by the one and only Doctor Lennon Hatch."

"What are you getting at?" Pavana questioned.

"That man was responsible for the explosion at the Konanavlah Sun Temple, a place well known in the scientific world as one of the most magnetic places on Earth."

Gita's mouth dropped open. "So you think the Sun Temple was an electron diffusion region, and that explosion had something to do with the magnetic poles flipping."

"Verse fifty-one!" Muni said triumphantly. "Only the Voices know the truth, and those who hear the Voices shall know New Earth."

"I don't understand," Gita said.

Muni glared at her, her piercing green eyes boring into Gita like lasers. "You only need to understand that the Sun Temple was a permanent X-Point. That money-grubbing, imbecilic fool Hatch went and got it destroyed. Therefore, he unknowingly opened the door to New Earth, much to our good fortune. Latitude 29.5347° N and longitude 35.4079° E is the location of a potential *new* permanent X-Point."

"What does this mean?" Pavana asked.

"It means we have to keep that X-Point from opening and stabilizing Earth's magnetic field. Otherwise the door to New Earth may close forever."

Gita looked Muni directly in the eyes. "And how in the world do you propose we accomplish that?"

Muni turned away from her without a response. She tilted back her head, closed her eyes, and whispered the missing final verse to *The Way to New Earth*.

Chapter Twenty-One
AXEL

Axel landed face-first into a mound of hot sand. He sat up, wiped the grit from his eyes, and saw Charu. She was a few yards away on her hands and knees, gagging from their sudden blast through the Warp.

He thought of Daisha. Usually she was the one Warping with him.

"Are you okay?" Axel asked.

Tears streamed down Charu's cheeks. "Where... what...just happened to me?"

"We went through the Warp."

"What does that even mean?"

"Well, according to Megan, the Warp works by dematerializing the elemental composition of our bodies via the solar wind and turning them into a stream of charged particles. The GeoPort then reconstitutes those particles back to our human form."

Charu sat up and wiped her mouth. "So, you're basically saying we were broken up into tiny pieces and sent flying across the world?"

Axel nodded. "Yep. That's the way it works."

"But I thought you said your GeoPort only functions with your DNA. How am I here?"

"Umm...yeah, I don't know. I don't think that's ever happened before. We were touching when it went off, so maybe that's how we Warped together. Think about it. Five minutes ago we were in India, and now we're at latitude 29.5347° N and longitude 35.4079° E."

Charu looked at the numbers on the GeoPort. "And where is that?"

Axel shrugged. A dry, seemingly endless desert stretched into the horizon. Strange rock formations jutted high into the sky. Intense heat beat down on them.

"I think we landed on Mars," Charu said, only half joking.

The skin on the back of Axel's neck began to sizzle with burn. "We have to get out of the sun," he said. "We could easily die out here."

Charu pointed toward two large rock formations not far away. They came together to form a kind of gorge.

"We might find some shade there," she said.

Axel nodded, and they started trekking over a

massive dune. He noticed two sets of faint footprints in the sand. They were heading in the same direction of the rock formations.

"This looks like a good sign," Axel said, showing Charu the prints. "Someone else must've had the same idea as us."

The rock formations were a lot farther away than they thought. It took them well over an hour to reach them, but the hike was worth the effort. The stone knolls blocked out the sun, giving them a welcomed respite from the heat.

"The footsteps go farther into the gorge," Axel said. "Do you want to follow them some more?"

Charu nodded. "Yes. It's probably cooler the deeper we go."

They rested another few minutes and started walking. Axel noticed very large animal hoofprints in the sand alongside the human footprints. Prehistoric illustrations of animals and people appeared on the walls.

"Look," Axel said. "Those petroglyphs look almost exactly like the ones back at the rock shelter in India."

"Fascinating," Charu said. "The animals appear to be horses and deer with very long horns."

"I wonder what the weird circles and wiggly lines mean?"

"Perhaps some kind of ancient script or religious symbol."

A dripping sound caught Axel's attention. "Do you hear that?" he asked.

"Sounds like water!" Charu exclaimed

They ran toward the sound. Their eyes lit up when they saw drips of liquid trickling from the rock walls and into a small puddle below. Both of them knelt down, splashing their faces and necks with the cool water.

"I'm dying of thirst," Axel said. "Should we drink?"

"It smells clean enough," Charu said. "And rocks are good filters, but..."

Axel didn't wait for her to finish. He cupped a handful of water and slurped it into his mouth. He was about to drink more, but Charu stopped him.

"That's enough," she said. "If the water's bad, it won't take long for you to start reacting. Let's wait and see how your stomach takes it."

They waited thirty minutes until Axel had to go to the bathroom. Since the water had gone through his system and he hadn't gotten sick, they figured the water in the puddle was safe to drink. They both swallowed several gulps. With their parched throats temporarily satisfied, they leaned against the cool rocks.

"When the sun goes down, we can start to look for

civilization," Axel said. "Maybe there are more foot-prints in the sand."

Charu splashed water in her face. "I hope we don't run into Minecraft zombies," she joked.

Axel laughed. "If there are zombies in this desert, we're dead meat."

Their moment of lighthearted humor quickly gave way to the reality of the situation. They were lost in an un-forgiving landscape where death at the hands of the extreme climate could happen at any moment. So they sat there and waited, both of them lost in their own thoughts as the hours went by. There was a dramatic drop in temperature, but that fact didn't give them much solace.

"Where are we?" Charu said, a dejected tone in her voice.

"A desert."

"But *which* desert?"

Axel scratched his head. "Let's see. How many deserts are there in the world? Sahara, Mojave, Arabian. Then there's the Chihuahuan Desert in Mexico. What's the one in Mongolia?"

"Gobi," Charu answered. "There's the Great Victoria Desert in Australia and Patagonia in Argentina. The largest desert in the world is Antarctica."

"We can definitely rule that one out."

Charu stood up, stretched, and paced around the gorge. After taking another drink of water, she ran her fingers lightly over the petroglyphs, retracing the artist's handiwork from thousands of years ago.

"This animal looks like a camel," she said. "That means we have to be in northern Africa, the Middle East, or Mongolia."

"Great," Axel said, his eyelids fluttering with fatigue. "If we're in the Middle East, I'll take a hummus platter, lamb kebabs, and a cold glass of iced tea."

Another petroglyph caught Charu's attention, one that someone had carved directly above Axel's head. She hadn't noticed it before, but they were modern numerals and not some ancient cryptic symbol. Below the numbers were six English letters.

Charu read the numbers aloud. "21.52, 75.3, 78.14, 0.9786."

"What are you mumbling?" Axel asked.

"D-A-I-S-H-A."

"Why are you spelling out Daisha's name?"

"Look above your head."

Axel glanced up at the wall and nearly burst out in tears. Scrawled crudely into the stone were:

21.52, 75.3, 78.14, 0.9786
DAISHA

Chapter Twenty-Two
DAISHA

Daisha rolled over, stretched, and opened her eyes. A brilliant orange sunrise peeked over the rocky outcrops. Loosha was sleeping next to her, softly snoring. The events of the previous day flooded back to her, from Warping to a barren desert in the Middle East and seeking shelter from the sun inside the rock crevice to Yaseen and the lost camel.

A short man who Khaled called Omar placed two bowls of yogurt drizzled with honey and a large plate of cherry tomatoes and cucumbers next to them.

"Thanks," Daisha said, sitting up on her elbows.

"*Bi kulli surur,*" Omar said and returned to the outdoor kitchen.

The smell of food nudged Loosha awake. He yawned, rubbed his eyes, and checked for the pistol he had hidden inside his boot.

"I have something to tell you," Loosha said. "It's been weighing on my mind for a while now."

"What?" Daisha asked, handing him a bowl of yogurt.

"You probably won't believe me, but I'm not the one who killed your mother at the dog park. It was my old partner, Kostia. I'm sorry it happened."

A lump formed in Daisha's throat, but she fought the urge to cry. Deep down, she knew Loosha was telling her the truth.

"Better eat this food," she said. "It may be a long time before we eat again."

"What does your GeoPort say?" Loosha asked, shoving a spoonful of yogurt into his mouth.

Daisha pulled the unit from her pocket. "21.52, 75.3, 78.14, 0.9786," she said. "Just like yesterday."

"Just get me out of this godforsaken place. I don't want to spend one more second here than I have to."

"Better count your blessings. Here we have hospitality and food. The next place could be much worse."

Loosha didn't argue with her. He plopped a couple cherry tomatoes in his mouth and stood up. Daisha did the same. Several tourists emerged from their tents. They ate breakfast at a long table. Two women waited on them while Yaseen and another boy rounded up the camels. Khaled stepped out of the tent and walked toward Daisha and Loosha.

"I hope you had good rest," Khaled said with a smile.

"Wonderful," Daisha replied. "We can't thank you enough for the food and ride this morning."

Khaled's smile faded away. "About that ride," he said, almost apologetically. "I originally had told you we can take you in the morning. That will not be possible, as we need the vehicles. However, we can take you this afternoon when we drop this tour group off at the Wadi Rum Visitor Center."

Loosha expelled a disappointed grunt.

"I'm sorry," Khaled said. "We will treat you as guests. You can come on the camel tour with us this morning. Free of charge."

Daisha sighed. "We really don't have a choice, do we?"

"Okay," Loosha said. "But I'll pay. I don't like owing anybody anything."

Khaled motioned them to follow him to the camel corral. Ten tourists were already mounted and ready to ride when they got there. Yaseen and the other boy led two large camels over to them.

"Who wants to ride this one?" Yaseen asked.

"That's the camel from yesterday," Daisha said. "I recognize the white spot on its hump."

Yaseen stroked the camel's neck. "This one is my

favorite, even though she likes to wander far in the night."

"You take that one," Loosha said. "That mangy monster spit in my face, and I want nothing to do with it."

Daisha giggled at the memory. "A reason to ride her even more," she said. "How are you supposed to get on these creatures?"

The camel knelt down, and Daisha mounted its back. Loosha did the same. Daisha had ridden horseback before, and this felt very similar. Loosha, on the other hand, looked like a fish out of water. His eyes bugged out. He gripped the reigns so hard his knuckles turned white.

The tour took up the whole morning. Khaled led them through the stunningly beautiful desert to a place called Lawrence's Spring. Daisha thought the place would be a cool, refreshing oasis, but the spring was nothing more than a puddle in the otherwise broiling desert. They then headed to Khazali Canyon to see inscriptions dating back more than two thousand years. After a jaunt through the mountains to a place called Small Rock Bridge, they headed back to the campsite.

The cargo van was waiting for them. After a lunch of pita bread and the yummiest hummus Daisha had ever tasted, they hopped in the back of the van with the tourists. The two-hour ride took them through some of the most beautiful desert scenery Daisha had ever seen.

"The landscape is so dramatic," Daisha said. "It's no wonder we thought this was the Grand Canyon."

"I don't like it here at all," Loosha said, staring out the window. "There's something haunted and dangerous that I can't put my finger on."

"Like what?"

"Forget about it. Just let me know when the GeoPort says it's time to fly."

Several stone buildings the same color as the surrounding mountains came into view. Inscribed on the largest building were the words *Wadi Rum Visitor Center* in both English and Arabic. Dozens of people meandered around the center. Some were Jordanian workers dressed in traditional garb, others obvious European and Asian tourists. The driver opened the doors and pointed to the parking lot where several buses sat idling in the heat.

"You can get all transportation to Petra, Amman, and the airports. Make sure you have your passes available."

The other passengers seemed to know exactly what bus line they were taking. Daisha and Loosha had no idea, so they inquired inside the visitor center.

They purchased two tickets to Aqaba on a bus called JETT, not scheduled to depart for another forty-five minutes.

Loosha loitered among the shops in the cool air-conditioning while Daisha waited outside. The scenery was so breathtaking that she wanted to soak in as much as possible before leaving. A large mountain with soaring pinnacles of red rock loomed on the horizon. Streaks of lightning flashed across the sky. A tourist leaflet about the mountain read: *Seven Pillars of Wisdom: famous landmark, named after the book by T. E. Lawrence.*

The GeoPort in Daisha's pocket buzzed to life. The familiar beeping sounds indicating the Warp had reset filled her ears. She pulled out the unit. Much to her surprise, the screen was blank. The numbers 21.52, 75.3, 78.14, 0.9786 were not flashing as usual.

"Does this mean what I think it means?" she asked. She started entering the coordinates for Hoover Park back in Palo Alto.

37.4302° N, 122.1288° W

She held her thumb over the SW button, tears rolling down her cheeks. She was amazed the GeoPort appeared to be working like normal. With a single press, she'd be back in Palo Alto and away from Loosha. But she knew Axel and Megan would not be there. They were somewhere in this vast desert. Deep down she knew that's why the GeoPort had sent her here in the first place. She deleted the coordinates and slipped the GeoPort back in her pocket.

Two JETT buses pulled into the parking lot, followed by an expensive-looking SUV with tinted windows.

Dozens of people departed the buses. All of them were women. Some carried little girls. They walked barefoot, wearing long white robes with flowers tucked behind their ears. However, the oddest thing about them was the weird-looking tattoo in the center of their foreheads.

The SUV with the tinted windows wheeled up beside Daisha. Three women stepped from the vehicle. Two were young, one was older, and they were dressed exactly like the people in the buses. White robes, barefoot, forehead tattoo, and all.

"Two in youth will guide you," the older woman mumbled and walked over to her. She had long gray hair and intense green eyes that burned directly into Daisha's soul.

"But they will not hear the Voices," she continued. "Only one of you will survive."

"Huh?" Daisha questioned. "Are you talking to me?"

With a nod from the older woman, the two younger ones grabbed Daisha roughly by the arms.

"Let me go!" Daisha screamed.

The older woman opened the SUV's door, and the women tossed her into the back seat. Seconds later, they raced out of the parking lot and down a dusty desert road.

Chapter Twenty-Three
MUNI

The SUV sped through the desert as Muni, Gita, and Pavana fought hard to subdue the girl in the back seat.

"Let me go!" the girl screamed, kicking and flailing with all her might.

"Climb atop the Seven Pillars of Wisdom, where New Earth awaits," Muni chanted.

"Two in youth will guide you, but they will not hear the Voices," Pavana added.

"Only one of you will survive," chimed Gita, completing the final verse of *The Way to New Earth*. Muni had finally revealed the prophetic words to them during the ride from the airport.

"Leave me alone!" the girl yelled as she reached up and scratched Pavana's cheek.

"Owww!" Pavana yelped, pinning the girl's arms with her knees.

The driver looked through the rearview mirror, a concerned look on his face *"Ma bika?"* he asked.

Muni had no idea what he was saying. She just smiled, pointed to the girl, and made the international symbol for crazy by twirling a finger around the side of her head.

This seemed to satisfy the driver. He nodded and turned his attention back to driving.

The three of them held the girl down as she thrashed and cried out some more, but the three grown women were too much for her. After another minute of intense wrestling, all the fight seeped out of her. She fell limp and exhausted within their grasp. Muni studied the girl's face with all the reverence of a cherished religious object. This young girl was without a doubt the same person from her vision, right down to the shorn head and wide, bright eyes.

"What do you want from me?" the girl asked, panting for breath.

"I knew exactly who you were when I first glimpsed you in the parking lot," Muni said. "Where's the boy?"

The girl didn't answer.

"She asked you about the boy!" Pavana hollered in the girl's face.

Muni shot Pavana a stern look. "Pavana, don't yell at

her like that. She's a gift from the Voices and must be treated with veneration and respect." She turned back to the girl. "Don't worry, my vision. You are one of the Antakaale's guides to New Earth. The Voices will make sure no harm comes to you."

They drove in silence for many miles before arriving at a large encampment. Dozens of tents and herds of wandering camels stretched along the horizon. A handful of native men and woman dressed in traditional attire were waiting for them.

The SUV screeched to a stop.

"Keep her here while I settle the arrangements," Muni said as she opened the door.

A tall man wearing a white keffiyeh draped loosely around his neck and shoulders approached her. Two women dressed in all black stood at his side.

"Welcome to our Hafnawi's Desert Life Camp!" the man said enthusiastically. "You are the..." The man looked down at a card. "Anta...kaale party, and there are eighty-seven of you, counting children, correct?"

Muni nodded. "Everyone should arrive shortly. They're not far behind."

"Perfect. My name is Fahd, and this is my wife, Ghazal, and our daughter, Tala. We are pleased to have you as our guests."

"I'm Muni. You'll deal directly with my assistants, Pavana and Gita, or me. No one else."

Fahd smiled. "Certainly. We have plenty of activities and daily excursions into Wadi Rum. We'll make your vacation as pleasant and fun as possible."

"Your entire party is female, correct?" Ghazal asked.

"Yes," Muni answered.

"Then we won't have to worry about any separate facilities. Please, join Tala and me. We'll show you the accommodations."

Hafnawi's Desert Life Camp was the largest tourist camp in Wadi Rum and the closest to the Seven Pillars of Wisdom. This is exactly why Muni chose it to be their starting ground for the exit to New Earth. The tents were set up to form a large semicircle with the openings facing away from the rising sun. Muni peeked in one of the tents and saw six basic cots made up with pillows and blankets, two stools with water basins, and six folding chairs. A much larger, circus-like tent was for dining and a common area. Ten tented bathrooms with showers sat behind a large jutting rock.

"This is your *khayma*," Ghazal said, parting the flaps of a tent marked number two. "*Khayma* is the word for 'tent' in Arabic. Number two's set far apart from the other tents for privacy, and it has more comforts."

Muni looked at her accommodations. Ghazal's idea of more comforts was three queen-size beds with fluffy comforters and fancy headboards. A large dresser filled with clean towels sat off to the side. Exquisite Persian rugs covered the floor, and a comfortable couch with a coffee table sat in the center.

"Very nice," Muni said. "There will be three of us in this tent, and we would like the utmost privacy."

The rumble of two large tour buses echoed outside.

"That must be the rest of your party," Ghazal said. "I must go greet them. I assure your privacy."

She left the tent. Muni stood there, staring blankly into space. A loud buzzing sound like that of a bumblebee vibrated in her ears. She knew the signal all too well. The Voices were coming.

Verse thirty-two of the Voices teachings echoed in her mind.

"The Voices speak in visions of the night," Muni whispered. "Their utterances reveal the mystery, the secret, the truth."

She closed her eyes tight and raised her arms in the air, accepting their invitation. A cool, calm breeze blew across her face. The tingling sensations came, like someone lightly stroking their fingertips over her bare skin.

The Voices were inside her mind.

Muni's heart pounded as she awaited their loving guidance. But this time their embrace wasn't warm and loving. Instead of gentle hugs, a sudden pain sliced through her skull. Her insides quaked, her knees buckled, and she fell to the ground. Flickering images of the hot desert raced through her mind. She felt intense heat and whipping sand stinging her face. In the vision, she was standing on the Seven Pillars of Wisdom with her followers in the background. She looked out at the vast emptiness and watched the door to New Earth appear in the clouds. The entryway was a shimmering tunnel of light like a billion stars in the sky. Triumphant feelings of euphoria filled her soul. She reached out to grab the golden handle, but it was just out of reach. The earth beneath her feet began to tremble and quake. Her followers cried out in anguish.

The girl from the car materialized out of the invisible essence. She watched as the girl reached into her pocket and pulled out a glowing Golden Jewel. The thing was magical, so much so that even the Voices flinched at its ferocious power.

"Two," the girl said. "We only need two."

"Two what?" Muni asked, her voice quivering with desperation.

Another image appeared, hovering on the horizon like a setting sun.

"The brown-haired boy," Muni gasped, remembering him from her previous vision.

Muni watched the boy reach into his pocket. He pulled out a matching Glowing Jewel. The boy winked at the girl. Together, they converged the two jewels into one giant laser beam. With a press of a button, the laser blew away the door to New Earth, closing it forever.

Chapter Twenty-Four
DAISHA

Daisha wanted to claw out the eyes of the two women holding her down. She felt she could take the one with the shaved head. The one called Pavana, however, might make a tougher fight.

"Where are you taking me?" Daisha said when the SUV started moving again.

"Don't you worry about it," Pavana said, lightly touching the scrape on her face. "If I weren't a woman of peace, I'd make you hurt for scratching me like this."

Daisha glared at her. "Do women of peace make a habit of snatching kids off the street?"

Pavana didn't answer.

Daisha looked up at the other woman. She had deep brown eyes and a shaved head. Several semi-healed scratches crisscrossed the tattoo on her forehead. The woman glanced at her. A quick smile flashed across her face and then faded.

"What's your name?" the lady with the shaved head asked her.

"Daisha," she spat. "Are you happy now?"

"My name's Gita," the woman responded. "And this is Pavana. The other woman is our leader, Muni. We don't want to hurt you."

"Then what do you want from me?"

The SUV came to a stop. The driver pointed to a tent marked number two, indicating this was where they should get out. Daisha's heart pumped with adrenaline. The second the door opened, she was going to scream at the top of her lungs and break away from her captors. Unfortunately, her plan quickly came to a grinding halt when Pavana pulled out a handkerchief, gagged Daisha's mouth, and secured her wrists and ankles with zip ties.

Pavana handed the concerned-looking driver a wad of Jordanian dinar. Gita opened the door. They heaved Daisha inside the tent. Muni was writhing on the floor, tears in her eyes. They tossed Daisha on one of the beds and ran to her.

"Muni!" Pavana cried. "What's wrong?"

"Are you sick?" Gita added.

"The Voices speak in visions of the night," Muni

hushed. "Their utterances reveal the mystery, the secret, the truth."

"Verse thirty-two," Pavana and Gita uttered in unison.

Muni sat up and wiped the tears away. She stared at Daisha, an intense glare that sent daggers into her chest. Daisha scowled back at her through the mouth gag. A deep hatred for the woman came over her. The word popped into her mind: *cult*.

Daisha's thoughts cried out. This is a cult! Some freaky, tattoo-in-the-center-of-the-forehead cult kidnapped me!

Panic pulsed through Daisha's body. Her stomach tightened, sweat beaded her forehead. She wiggled on the bed, desperately trying to free herself from the bindings. It was no use. The harder she fought, the deeper the zip ties dug in to her skin.

Muni walked over to her and sat down on the bed. "Where's the boy?" she asked.

Daisha mumbled something incoherent through the gag.

"If you scream when I take this off, you'll spend your entire time with me wearing a gag," Muni warned. "Besides, we are set far apart from the other tents. No one will hear you anyway. Do we have a deal?"

Daisha nodded, and Muni removed the gag from her mouth. She gasped, sucking a deep and welcomed breath into her lungs.

"What do you want?" Daisha huffed.

"She told you already," Pavana said. "Where's the boy?"

"If you're talking about Loosha, he's back at the visitor center," Daisha said.

"Is that his real name?"

"Yes."

Muni looked at Pavana. "Bring him to me. Find the driver and give him plenty of dinar to keep quiet. There's a stun gun in my bag. Use it if necessary. Go. Now!"

Pavana raced outside and into the hot sun. Muni and Gita moved to the far end of the tent, whispering among themselves. Daisha strained her ears to hear what they were saying. Three of their words made her heart freeze.

Electron. Diffusion. Region.

How could they possibly know about that? She listened some more, catching scraps of their conversation. She heard things like *magnetic poles*, *flipping*, *earthquakes*, *geophysics*, and *New Earth*. None of it made sense to her.

Muni walked over to the bed, reached into Daisha's pocket, and pulled out the GeoPort. The unit pulsed with blue starbursts.

"The Golden Jewel of my vision," Muni said, cradling the GeoPort between her palms. "The boy named Loosha has the other. We need to destroy both of them so the door to New Earth will open."

"It's called a GeoPort," Daisha said. "Not a *Golden Jewel.*"

"May I?" Gita asked.

Muni handed her the GeoPort.

A voice called from outside the tent.

"*Marhaba?* Hello?"

Before Daisha could cry out, Muni quickly tied the gag back around her mouth.

"Who is it?" Muni asked.

"It's Tala," a female voice answered. "My father sent me. He needs to speak with you quickly about some of the arrangements and activities."

"One moment." She turned to Gita. "Watch her."

Muni slipped a lotus flower behind her ear and left the tent. Gita peeked through the flap, watched her walk away with Tala, and then removed the gag from Daisha's mouth.

"This is a fascinating piece of equipment you have

here," Gita said, studying the GeoPort. "What do you use it for?"

"None of your business," Daisha said. "Just give it back. I'm the only one who can use it anyway."

Gita pressed the SW button. Nothing happened.

"Tell me your last name and where you're from," Gita said. "Then I'll think about giving it back to you."

"My name's Daisha Tandala. I'm from Palo Alto, California. Now give it back!"

A surprised look washed over Gita's face. "Did you say *Tandala*?"

Daisha nodded.

"Are you related to Jodiann Tandala? She's a professor at Stanford."

Daisha lurched, like Gita had just sucker punched her in the gut. How in the world could this crazy cult devotee know her mother's name?

"She's my mother," Daisha said. "Someone shot her."

The woman's response surprised Daisha. A wellspring of tears burst from her eyes. She plopped down on the bed.

"Did you know her?" Daisha asked.

"No, but I've heard her name many times. My real name's..."

Gita's voice trailed off, like she wasn't sure if trusting

Daisha was the right thing to do.

"They call you Gita," Daisha pressed. "Isn't that your real name?"

Gita shook her head. "I'm Luciana...Lopez. I was a professor of geophysics at Caltech. The Antakaale have my—"

Daisha sensed an opening and pounced. "Anta... what?"

"That's the name of our group. They have my little daughter, Varya...Catalina."

"And they're holding her over your head, aren't they?" Daisha wiggled closer to her. "You don't want to be here as much as I do. You're a hostage just like me. Untie me. We'll find your daughter and get out of this place."

Gita wiped away her tears and produced a pocketknife from a backpack. She sliced the zip ties from Daisha's wrists. Just as she was about to snip the restraints from Daisha's ankles, the tent flap flew open and Muni stepped inside.

Chapter Twenty-Five
AXEL

The sun beat down on Axel and Charu as they walked deeper into the desert. They had slurped enough water from the puddle to make their bellies bulge, but it was not enough to keep the intense temperature at bay.

"I need to rest," Charu groaned. Her face was flushed, her breathing slow and labored.

"Just a little farther," Axel said as he trudged over a sand dune. "These prints have to be from Daisha. She's been here. She's alive."

"What prints?"

Axel looked to the ground. The footprints they had been following were gone, covered up by the wind and sand.

"We're going in the right direction," he said.

"How do you know?"

He yanked the GeoPort from his pocket. The

coordinates 29.5347° N, 35.4079° E flickered on the screen in neon green. When he had seen Daisha's name and the numbers scrawled on the wall, he could barely contain his excitement. Now, an hour into their trek into the dry expanse of desert, he regretted leaving the gorge and puddle of water.

"We have to keep walking," Axel said.

They continued trudging into the wall of heat. Sweat poured down their faces. Axel gripped his hamstring. His wound had healed significantly, but his legs were cramping and a throbbing headache pounded in his skull.

"Are you okay?" Charu asked.

Axel didn't answer her. A sudden spell of dizziness came over him, and he dropped to one knee. Charu ran to him.

"Heat exhaustion," she said. "I've seen this many times in India. You're not used to this temperature."

"I'm fine," Axel said, standing back up. "We need to keep going. Daisha's here somewhere, and I have to find her."

After resting for a moment on the shady side of an outcrop, they trudged farther into the sand. Axel took a few steps and looked into the sky. Streaks of brilliant colors danced and twinkled on the horizon.

"What is that?" he asked.

Charu looked up, her eyes wide with astonishment. "I've never seen anything like that in my life."

"It looks like the aurora borealis."

The borealis disappeared and the wind picked up. Grit and dust blew in Axel's and Charu's eyes and mouths. They turned their backs, but the gusts were coming at them in all directions. Several whirling funnels appeared in the distance.

"Sand devils," Axel said. "And they're coming our way."

The visibility dropped dramatically. Axel tried to take a step forward but couldn't move. He looked down. Sand was now covering him and Charu to the calves, slowly burying them alive.

"We're not going to make it!" Charu cried out.

That's when Axel saw two sets of giant eyeballs coming at them. His insides froze in terror. A giant sand monster was about to eat Charu and him like a real-life horror movie. The eyeballs stopped right before them. He heard two loud bangs like car doors slamming. Strange voices echoed along with the hissing wind.

"*Yalla!*" a man's deep voice called. "Get them inside!"

That's when Axel saw two men. They wore

red-and-white checkered headdresses and dark green army-like uniforms with patches on the chest. One man grabbed Axel, the other Charu, and pulled them from the sand. A few steps later and they were in the back seat of a four-wheel drive Nissan SUV.

Relief from being out of the sandstorm was instant. Axel and Charu coughed, hacking up grit and dirt from their lungs. The driver revved the engine, spun the wheels a few times, and sped off into the desert. A patch on their shirt read *Wadi Rum Desert Patrol*.

The man in the front passenger's seat passed them a water bottle. Axel and Charu took turns chugging until the bottle was empty. After a few minutes of driving, they were out of the sandstorm and into the bright sunshine.

"You're lucky we saw you before the storm hit," the driver said, peering into the back seat through the rearview mirror. "You could have died out here."

"How'd you get separated from your party?" the other man asked in a thick accent.

Axel didn't quite know how to answer. After all, he couldn't tell the man that he and Charu had Warped there and didn't have a party. Finally, he just nodded yes.

"What camp are you visiting?" asked the driver.

A glossy, trifold tourist brochure was sitting between them in the back seat.

Charu scooped it up and blurted, "We want to go back to the visitor center."

The driver nodded, turned the SUV around, and sped in the opposite direction. An hour later, stone buildings came into view. A sign read *Wadi Rum Visitor Center*.

Axel and Charu thanked the men and stepped from the SUV. They saw tour buses, a few local workers dressed in robes and headdresses, and dozens of tourists. They opened the door to the visitor center to a blast of cool air-conditioning. People stared at them as they took turns slurping from the water fountain.

"You're a grimy mess," Axel told Charu.

"And you look like you just took a bath in a pile of dirt," said Charu. "Let's wash off and meet back here."

Axel pushed open the men's room door and looked in the mirror. He was filthy. The sun exposure had burned his face red. Dirt, muck, and sand covered every inch of his exposed skin. He turned on the water and splashed his face, arms, and neck. There were no paper towels, so he air-dried himself.

The handle of the toilet stall jiggled, and a large man with a bull tattoo on his neck stepped out. They looked at each other. After a confused moment, both of their faces flashed with recognition.

"Loosha!" Axel cried and burst out of the bathroom.

Chapter Twenty-Six
MEGAN

The airplane's sudden drop in altitude made Megan's stomach lurch into her esophagus. She grabbed Jag's hand as the turbulence rocked the plane back and forth. Flying had always made her nervous, but this flight from New Delhi to Aqaba, Jordan, felt like climbing inside a metal garbage can and tumbling down the Grand Canyon.

A male voice echoed throughout the cabin from the intercom: "Please return to your seats and fasten your seat belts."

Seat belts clicked and passengers stumbled back to their seats. Flight attendants scurried up and down the aisle collecting garbage. A baby one row over started crying. The mother popped a bottle in the infant's mouth. An overhead compartment flew open, and a large carry-on crashed to the floor.

"It'll be okay," Jag said, trying to reassure her. "Just a little turbulence, that's all."

Megan looked out the window, saw the left wing shaking, and quickly closed the shade. The flight had been rocky from takeoff, but she and Jag had no other choice. After cell service came back up in India, Megan googled the coordinates 29.5347° N, 35.4079° E. She discovered they were for a place called the Wadi Rum desert in Jordan, and she knew that's where Axel and Charu had Warped. A sneaking suspicion also told her that Daisha might be there.

"I think I'm going to throw up," Megan said.

"Do you need the barf bag?" Jag asked.

Megan shook her head. "Not yet, but I'm working on it."

"Why do I feel like I'm in a disaster movie?" a middle-aged businessman sitting behind them joked.

His comment made the surrounding passengers chuckle, but given what had happened in recent days, everyone seemed particularly on edge. Megan knew that if she and Jag didn't find Axel, Daisha, and the two GeoPorts, this disaster movie would be all too real.

A female voice blasted over the intercom. "Flight attendants and cabin crew, please be seated. Ladies and gentlemen, this is your captain, Perri Towles. We are now passing over a very large hurricane in the Arabian Sea that's causing a lot of turbulence. We should be swimming out of it shortly. However, we've just received a radio transmission about seven, yes, you heard me right, seven hurricanes being reported around the globe. This may affect your connecting flights. Please check with your airline when we land in Aqaba. Thank you for flying Oceana."

A flight attendant then repeated the message in another language. Megan looked at Jag, her eyes filled with worry. "Seven hurricanes. Can you believe it? If we don't create a new X-Point soon, the world as we know it ends."

"We'll land safely in Aqaba and find the kids," Jag said. "I just know it. Why don't you try and get some sleep? You'll need every ounce of energy to pull this off."

Sleep was the last thing on Megan's mind. The plane seemed to steer out of the turbulence and stabilize, making her stomach feel much better. She took a deep breath and rummaged in the seat pocket. There was the standard safety instruction material, barf bag, and an in-flight magazine called *Oceana and You*. She was just about to pick it up when another magazine called *Science Sphere* caught her eye. The cover story was about some modern-day doomsday cult. On the cover was a slightly blurry picture—obviously taken from a long-lens camera—of a gray-haired woman with a crazy tattoo on her forehead wearing a long white robe.

The caption read: *From Geophysics Superstar to Cult Leader: The Story of Benedykta Wójcik, PhD.*

A slice of intense déjà vu rippled through Megan's stomach. "How do I know this woman?" she wondered, turning to the article.

The magazine went into detail about Benedykta Wójcik—her modest beginnings on a farm in Poland, professorship at Caltech, and winning the coveted Vetlesen Prize in geophysics. The story became seriously strange after that. The author of the article interviewed some of Benedykta's former colleagues. All of them claimed her behavior became erratic within months after winning the Vetlesen.

"Benny—that's what everyone called her back then—started claiming to hear voices, see visions," Sara Hanson, PhD, Wójcik's former research assistant, says. "She abandoned her husband and only child. Sadly, the woman was obviously descending into the ravages of paranoid schizophrenia. We in the department tried getting her help from doctors and medication. But she refused our offers and disappeared almost overnight."

Another colleague, Hugo Cyr, PhD, says, "About a year after she left the university, I received a strange little pamphlet in the mail from her. Only she had started calling herself Muni by that time. The booklet was filled with these odd, disturbing, pseudo-religious verses. Obviously the product of a diseased, schizophrenic mind."

Megan studied the accompanying photograph. The pamphlet was named *The Way to New Earth*, and the group she had founded called themselves the Antakaale, a Sanskrit term meaning "the end of life."

The article picked up many years later, when the author tracked her to a tea plantation in Sri Lanka. By this time, she had nearly one hundred followers and a bank account in the millions. Megan's heart sunk when the desperate relatives of her followers joined the article. After the women fell under Muni's spell, they each wrote one last letter to their families in tiny, bizarre-looking script, saying their relatives were never going to hear from them again. As far as the women were concerned, Muni and the Voices were their real and only family.

> "I've spent virtually all my retirement nest egg on private investigators trying to find my daughter," says the father of Luciana Lopez, one of Muni's followers.
>
> "As far as I'm concerned, this Muni person is a criminal," Lopez's mother adds, wiping away tears. "A brainwashing, kidnapping criminal. She's a monster."

Megan glanced down the page and saw an old picture of a young Benedykta. She held a baby and stood next to a tall man with asphalt-black hair.

The caption read: *Benedykta abandoned her husband, noted geologist Russell Hollinger, and her daughter, Megan.*

Megan burst into tears.

"What's wrong?" Jag asked, taking her hand.

"This article...the woman in the picture. She's... my—"

"She's what?"

"Benedykta Wójcik is my mother!"

The plane rattled violently, dropping several thousand feet in altitude. The nose pointed nearly straight down. Cups, cans, and pieces of paper flew into the air. Noxious yellow smoke filled the cabin.

"What's happening?" the businessman next to them shouted.

"We're going down!" cried another passenger.

People screamed, a loud buzzer blasted around the cabin, and air masks dropped from the ceiling. The contents of Megan's airplane breakfast belched into her mouth. She leaned forward and vomited directly into the seat pocket.

Chapter Twenty-Seven
LOOSHA

Loosha took off after the boy. He burst from the bathroom and ran down the hallway past several local artisans' tables. A crowd of people jumped out of the way. He pushed open the doors of the visitor center and stepped outside. Where was he? The kid looked like Axel, but he wasn't yet sure. Then again, how did the kid know his name?

"Axel!" Loosha yelled out. "I'm here with Daisha! Come back!"

A large group of Asian tourists were approaching. Loosha weaved through them and ran around the side of the building to the parking lot. Three passenger vans wheeled past him. The boy was nowhere in sight.

"Axel!" Loosha hollered again. "I have Daisha!"

But where was Daisha? Before he had stepped into the visitor center to use the bathroom, she was standing right here in the parking lot. Now she was gone.

"Daisha! I saw Axel!"

There was no response. Loosha's cheeks flushed with anger. He shrugged off the emotion, knowing full well they couldn't have gone too far in this massive desert. The visitor center had several buildings. They were probably somewhere hiding among them. Or, maybe...

"The GeoPort," he said, interrupting his own thoughts. "What if it reset and they both Warped out of here? That means I'm stuck!"

Loosha quickly dismissed that scenario. The visitor center was small. If the kids had detonated into the Warp, he certainly would have heard the bang and seen the smoky electrical discharge. They had to be here somewhere.

"I'll find you!" he screamed. "Sooner or later!"

An Arab man approached him. Instead of the traditional outfit of robes and headdresses, he wore a camouflaged Jordanian military uniform with a red beret, thick utility belt, and shiny black boots.

"Can I help you with something, sir?" the man said. "Have you lost someone?"

Loosha reached for the gun hidden down the back of his pants but thought better of it. Finding out what had happened to Daisha and Axel was too important.

"Yes, actually," Loosha said. "Two people in my party seemed to have wandered off. One was a young black girl with very short hair. The other was a white boy with longish brown hair. Have you seen them?"

"I've seen him with a girl, but she wasn't black. Follow me."

Relief swelled in Loosha's chest. Where there was Axel, Daisha would not be far behind. The man led him to the other side of the parking lot to a set of stone steps. After a short climb, they were standing on a dirt road.

"He was just here, crouching by this big rock," the man said. "I saw him when I was on security patrol."

"Where could he have gone?" Loosha asked.

The man shrugged. "Either up the side of the hill where there is nothing but stones and sand or back to the visitor center."

Loosha scurried up the embankment. He looked around. There was no sign of Axel and nowhere for him to hide.

"He didn't go that way," Loosha said after he had climbed back down.

"Then he must have gone back to the visitor center," the man said and walked away.

An empty tour bus was idling in the parking lot.

Over the driver's objections, Loosha bullied his way into the bus and looked to see if the kids were hiding inside. There was no sign of them. He made his way back to the visitor center. The place was more crowded than before thanks to the tour bus and passenger vans. People crowded around the craft tables, buying handmade blankets, rugs, and other trinkets from the locals.

"Axel, Daisha!" Loosha bellowed. "This game you two are playing is old."

Loosha saw flash of long brown hair zip from behind the information kiosk and out the door. It was Axel. He was running with a girl, but it wasn't Daisha. A big smile spread across Loosha's face, and he raced to catch up. The chase took them through the tented reception area, down a stone path, and into the parking lot.

"Stop if you want to see Daisha again!" Loosha roared.

Axel and the girl stopped in their tracks and turned to Loosha.

"You're lying," Axel said, panting for breath.

"I'm far from lying, my friend," Loosha said back. "She's here somewhere. We've been Warping together all over the world. She's quite the traveling partner, I must say."

"Then where is she?"

"Just stay right there and I'll show you."

Loosha walked calmly toward him. Axel just glared at him. The girl was crying, tears streaming down her cheeks. When Axel was within arm's length, Loosha reached out and grabbed him roughly by the arm.

"Let him go!" the girl yelled.

"Shut up," Loosha growled, making the girl recoil. "I don't know who you are but get out of here. This is between him and me."

"I'm not going anywhere," the girl spat back.

Just as Loosha was about to lash out at her with his free arm, a car screeched to a stop right beside them. A strange-looking woman with long black hair and a funny-looking tattoo on her forehead stepped out of the car. She was barefoot and wore a white robe that billowed in the wind. A tall Arab man rolled down the window and joined her. A pamphlet fell from his pocket and fluttered across the parking lot.

"I'm looking for someone," the woman said.

"You and me both," Axel said back.

The woman looked at Axel. "Is your name Loosha?" she asked.

Axel shook his head. "My name's Axel. This guy's Loosha."

Loosha stared at her with wide eyes. "What do you want with me?"

"I've been sent for you. It's extremely urgent," the woman said.

"Why?"

The woman stepped closer. "Have you ever heard of a girl named Daisha?"

Both Loosha and Axel gasped out loud, not quite believing their ears.

"Say that again," Loosha said. "Very slowly."

"I said: Have you ever heard of girl named Daisha? She's looking for you."

Loosha smiled. "Take me to her. Now."

"My pleasure," the woman said as she yanked out what Loosha recognized instantly as a stun gun.

"Get away from—" Loosha growled.

Before he could utter another syllable, the woman shoved the stun gun into his side and sent one million volts of electricity directly into his nervous system.

Chapter Twenty-Eight
MUNI

Muni stared at the Seven Pillars of Wisdom from the encampment. The stunning, wind-sculpted mountain poked out of the red desert like stubby fingers reaching for the clouds. Her vision had been clear and powerful. New Earth would open its doors to the Antakaale on its highest summit, but only if she could keep both Golden Jewels away from the place.

Other than Daisha and Gita back at the tent, Muni was alone in their base camp. Pavana was bringing back the brown-haired boy, and the rest of her followers were on a two-hour camel ride excursion. Fahd and the rest of Hafnawi's Desert Life Camp crew had rounded everyone up after lunch, including the children. Muni hadn't told her followers why they were here other than for a vacation. The outings were to keep them entertained until the final ascent to New Earth.

A cloud of dust appeared in the distance. The SUV with Pavana and, hopefully, the brown-haired boy was approaching. The anticipation of possessing the second jewel sent tingles up Muni's spine. She had first heard those precious Voices over twenty years ago. Now, they were only a day or so away from fulfilling the final prophecy.

The SUV wheeled around behind the tent. Pavana and the driver hopped out. Muni quickly handed him a thick wad of dinar to keep his mouth shut.

"Did you find Loosha?" she asked.

"Yes," Pavana said. "Easily and without incident."

"Good."

Pavana motioned toward the back seat of the car. "Do you want to see him? He's still passed out from the stun gun."

"Not yet," Muni said. "I want to talk to Gita and Daisha first."

Muni stepped into their tent. Gita was standing over Daisha, cutting the zip ties from Daisha's wrists.

"Stop!" Muni ordered.

Gita leaped a foot into the air, her eyes wide with surprise.

"I...uh...um," she stuttered.

Muni ran to the bed, grabbed another zip tie, and

re-bound Daisha's wrists. She turned to Gita, raised her hand, and struck her hard across the face. Gita fell to the ground, tears in her eyes and a painful red welt forming on her cheek.

"You will never see Varya again!" Muni roared.

"Please," Gita begged. "I need to see her. She's my daughter."

"Gita wasn't doing anything wrong," Daisha said, trying to diffuse the situation. "She took the ties off so I could show her how to use the GeoPort. Don't you want to know how it works?"

Muni looked suspiciously at Gita, then to Daisha, and back to Gita again. Slowly, the rage melted off Muni's face. She ran a hand through her long gray hair and plucked the GeoPort off the bed.

"I want to know what you use this thing for," Muni asked. "And you better tell me the truth. The Voices are very afraid."

"Who or what are the Voices?" Daisha asked.

"You'll know their whisperings soon enough. Maybe after I destroy this thing they'll allow you entry into New Earth with us."

"Why would you destroy it? This unit's the greatest technological advancement known to mankind."

"Enlighten me," Muni demanded and listened

intently as Daisha reluctantly explained the inner workings of the GeoPort—Warps, DNA, the Doctor, Konanavlah Sun Temple, and X-Points.

"Daisha, you've just confirmed our theory," Gita said, slipping on her geophysicist hat. "We've already discussed this in detail. Destroying the permanent X-Point has destabilized Earth's magnetic field, making the poles start to flip. That's why all the earthquakes, tsunamis, volcanic eruptions are happening. So, if I'm getting this right, we need both of the Geo...er...Golden Jewels to make a new X-Point. Which is why—"

"There will be no new X-Point," Muni said, finishing Gita's sentence. "If a new permanent X-Point arises, the door to New Earth will close forever. The Voices have told me this." She closed her eyes and shouted, "Only the Voices know the truth, and those who hear the Voices shall know New Earth!"

The tent flap opened and Pavana stepped inside. "Verse fifty-one," she said proudly. "Are you ready for Loosha? I haven't checked his pockets for the second Golden Jewel. I wanted to give you that honor."

A wide smile spread across Muni's face. "Bring him to me," she commanded. "New Earth is almost upon us."

Pavana left and returned a moment later with

Loosha. She had tied his hands with zip ties and taken his gun away. He was very groggy and weak from repeated blasts from the stun gun but was able to walk clumsily on two feet. She nudged him to the ground and zip-tied his ankles.

"Here he is," Pavana said. "The one from your vision."

Muni's smile faded into a scowl. "This isn't the one from my vision. He was just a boy. With long curly brown hair, blue eyes. This lump is a grown man."

"Axel," Daisha said.

"Who?" Muni asked.

"You've just described my friend, Axel. He has the other GeoPort."

"I thought his name was Loosha," Pavana said.

"You asked me who I was with at the visitor center. That person was Loosha, not Axel."

Pavana's eyes grew wide. "I saw him," she said. "The boy was back at the visitor center with Loosha. He even said his name was Axel."

"Impossible," Daisha muttered.

"It's true! He had long brown hair, blue eyes, and everything."

"Then go back and get him," Muni ordered. "Bring him to me. The Voices won't wait for us forever."

Pavana raced out of the tent.

Muni turned to Gita. "Tell me verse sixty-two."

Gita cleared her throat and recited, "Young daughters are a gift from the Voices. We praise them for they hear the Voices clearly and without question."

"Do you hear the Voices clearly and without question?" Muni asked.

"Yes," Gita said, trying very hard to fight back tears.

"Varya is a gift from the Voices. Therefore, she belongs to the Voices and not to you. Do you understand this?"

A single tear rolled down Gita's cheek. "Yes, I understand."

"Say good-bye to her in your mind. The Voices command that you never see her again on this Earth."

Muni grabbed the GeoPort and left the tent, zipping the flaps closed behind her.

Chapter Twenty-Nine
DAISHA

Daisha watched as Gita collapsed on the floor in a puddle of tears. Her sobs reverberated around the tent—deep, guttural cries that came from the pit of her soul. She felt bad for the woman, but all she could think of was Axel.

"He's alive!" she shouted in glee.

Loosha stirred on the floor, mumbled something incoherently, and opened his eyes.

"Where am I?" he murmured.

"Inside a pretty fancy tent, *chłopak*," Daisha said. "Where'd you find Axel?"

"He was at the visitor center."

Several questions rolled out of Daisha's mouth one after another. "How'd he get there? Did he look okay? Was anyone with him? What can we do to get him?"

"First, answer this question for me, *dziewczyna*.

How'd you get here?"

Daisha told him about the three women who had approached her in the parking lot at the visitor center and how they shoved her in a car, tied her hands and ankles, and dragged her to this tent.

"Why do they want you?" Loosha wondered.

"They were after the GeoPort," Daisha answered. "But the gray-haired lady, the one named Muni, calls it a *Golden Jewel*. Now, tell me about Axel."

"Nothing much to tell. Accept for painful-looking sunburn on his face, he looked fine. He was with some girl."

"Was her name Megan? She's a white woman with dyed-black hair and a partially shaved head."

"The girl he was with wasn't a woman. She was around his age. And she wasn't white. My guess would be Indian or Pakistani. Some nationality like that."

Daisha wiggled herself to a seated position. She let out a painful squeal. The sharp plastic of the zip ties had dug deeper into her skin.

"But why would he be here?" she asked, talking more at herself than Loosha.

"Probably looking for you," Loosha said. "Like a lot of people seem to be doing."

Gita let out another round of excruciating wails. Her

sobbing had not subsided one bit since Muni had left. She still lay crumpled in the corner, desperate and forlorn, seemingly oblivious to the conversation going on around her.

Loosha rolled over, struggling with the zip ties. "What's with the cry baby?" he asked.

"She has a young daughter here somewhere," Daisha said. "I heard Muni say she was never going to see the child again."

"Why?"

"Because the woman is crazy, that's why! She keeps talking about this place called New Earth. They're waiting for some mystical door to open so they can all go there."

A massive gust of wind shook the tent. Thunder rumbled in the sky. Lightning flickered, reflecting against the canvas walls. She heard the squeals of several frightened camels followed by pounding hoofs in the sand.

"Listen to that!" Daisha squealed.

"Must be getting a big rainstorm soon," Loosha said.

"Are you kidding me? There probably hasn't been a drop of rain in this desert since Noah's Ark," said Daisha.

Gita sat up. She wiped her eyes and blew her nose

into a tissue. Her wailing had slowed to a snivel. Daisha's pulse raced. If she and Loosha wanted to escape and go look for Axel, Gita was the one who would have to free them.

There was another blast of thunder, followed by cracks of lightning. More heavy winds trembled the tent walls.

"I don't care what you say," Loosha said to Daisha. "A torrential downpour is coming."

"It's not a rainstorm," Gita said, staring hard at both of them. "It's the end of the world."

Daisha raised her eyebrows. "Excuse me?"

"I'll explain everything after I untie you two."

Gita rummaged around the tent until she found a knife. With four quick slices, Daisha and Loosha were free.

"Thank you," Daisha said, rubbing her wrists. "Those things were cutting off my circulation."

Loosha stood up, still wobbly from the stun gun attack. He quickly searched his pockets and the back of his pants. "They took my pistol," he said with a frown.

Daisha unzipped the tent and peeked out the flap. "Wow!" she said, her voice mixed with both fear and amazement. "Just...holy...Wow! You two have to see this."

The sky above their heads flashed red, green, orange, purple, and all of the colors in between. It was like some giant celestial artist had spilled his paints all over the ozone layer, and now the entire universe was dripping with color.

"It's...It's...beautiful," Loosha said with stunned awe.

"Amazing," Daisha hushed.

"Deadly," Gita said ominously. "Earth's magnetic poles are well into the process of flipping right before our eyes."

"I don't understand," Daisha said.

"The solar wind is causing the light show we're witnessing," Gita explained. "This is because Earth's magnetic field is growing thin. That field is what protects us from planet-killing radiation. Soon, possibly in a matter of hours, the magnetic poles will have flipped, and our magnetic safety net will be gone."

"And then we'll be dead," Loosha added.

Gita nodded. "Unless we can get both GeoPorts. Muni has one. I assume this Axel person has the other."

"You better start making sense," Daisha demanded.

"I'm saying that when Doctor what's-his-name destroyed the permanent X-Point at the Sun Temple, he unwittingly kicked into gear the destruction of our planet. The earth and sun need a permanent magnetic connection to each other. If that doesn't happen, this is the consequence. My instincts say we need *both* GeoPorts to create a new X-Point. How we do that is another question all together."

"Megan would know," Daisha said.

"Who's Megan?" Gita asked.

"No time to explain. Nothing happens unless we have both GeoPorts anyway."

"How do we get them?" Loosha asked.

Daisha paced the tent, thinking. "Okay, I got it," she said. "Loosha, you and Gita—"

"My real name's Luciana," Gita said, interrupting her. "If I'm going to die, it will be with my real name, not one Muni gave me."

"Luciana," Daisha said, correcting herself. "You two figure out a way to get the GeoPort and your daughter from Muni. I'll head back to the visitor center to get Axel. Where should we meet?"

Luciana pointed to the mountain in the distance. "We'll meet there, atop the Seven Pillars of Wisdom. That's where Muni and all her followers, including my Catalina, are going."

"Why there?" Loosha asked.

"That's where the door to New Earth will open."

"Good luck and see you soon," Daisha said and raced into the swirling sand.

Chapter Thirty
AXEL

"What just happened?" Charu asked, her mouth hanging open.

"I don't know," Axel said. "But why did a large man and a freaky woman with a tattoo on her forehead just tase Loosha, toss him into a car, and speed away?"

"Where do you think they're taking him?"

"Who knows? A piece of paper flew out of the driver's jacket. Maybe that will help."

Axel jogged across the parking lot, grabbed the piece of paper, and rejoined Charu.

"Does it say anything?" Charu asked.

"It's a brochure for a campground called Hafnawi's Desert Life Camp," Axel said. "There's a map and everything. It says the camp is only one hour by car from the visitor center. Price includes your choice of hot air balloon ride, camel tour, and guided hike. Additional activities extra."

"What do we do now?"

"Loosha said Daisha was here at the visitor center. We need to find her. If he wasn't lying, that means she's still alive!"

Axel could barely contain his excitement over seeing Daisha. He was getting so close. His heart pounded with anticipation as he and Charu spent the next hour calling her name and scouring every inch of the visitor center. Tour groups came and went, but not one trace of Daisha.

"She's not here," Axel groaned, leaning against a wall in the parking area. "He really was lying."

"She's not here, but maybe we can find her at Hafnawi's Desert Life Camp," Charu suggested.

"What are you saying?"

"If that woman and man took Loosha back to this camp then maybe Daisha is there too. They have both of them."

Axel's eyes widened with excitement, renewed hope of finding Daisha filling his soul. "You may be right," he said. "But how do we get there? We certainly can't walk there in this heat."

Charu nodded. "Yes. We tried hiking in the desert alone and with no supplies. We'd be dead right now if it weren't for the Wadi Rum Desert Patrol."

A door opened behind them and out walked a man dressed like he was in the Jordanian army. Axel and Charu had seen him before, when they were hiding from Loosha behind the big rock.

"What's all the commotion out here?" the man asked and looked hard at Axel. "Hey, you're that boy the man was looking for. He had a tattoo on his neck. Are you with the same tour group?"

Axel shrugged, not knowing what to say.

"Yes," Charu answered and grabbed the brochure from Axel's pocket. "We need to go to this place. That's where we're supposed to meet him."

The man looked at the pamphlet. "Of course, Hafnawi's Desert Life Camp," he said. "I know Fahd, the owner, very well."

"How can we get a ride there?" Axel asked.

"Next van comes in four hours," the man said, looking at his watch. "If one comes at all. From what I understand, Fahd's people already picked up a very large tour group. There may be no reason for them to come back."

"What do we do now?" Charu wondered.

"Wait here," the man suggested. "If a van doesn't come, inform the front desk and we'll make arrangements for you to sleep somewhere here."

The man went back inside the building, closing the door behind him.

"Well, at least they have a water fountain and bathroom," Charu said. "Perhaps they have a manicure salon and I could get my nails done while we wait."

"We need to find this campground now!" Axel shouted, not in the mood for joking. "If Daisha's really there, I need to know. Besides, she could be in trouble. Look what that woman did to Loosha with the stun gun."

The roar of loud motor engines caught their attention. They turned around and saw three jeeps cruising into the parking lot. A decal plastered on their driver's side-doors read *Wadi Rum Jeep Tours*. The vehicles were dusty and dirty, like they had just come back from a long drive. Three young Arab men hopped out of the jeeps and walked into the visitor center. Two of them turned off the jeeps. One left his running with the key in the ignition.

Axel and Charu looked at each other with sly grins.

"Are you thinking what I'm thinking?" Axel asked.

"Have you ever driven a standard vehicle before?" Charu asked back.

Axel shook his head. "The closest thing to a car with an engine I've driven was a go-cart at Disneyland."

Charu smiled. "I'm only fifteen, but I've driven plenty of vehicles in my day."

"Let's do it!"

Axel hopped into the passenger's seat. Charu slipped into the driver's side. She let go of the emergency brake, shifted from neutral to first gear, and zipped out of the parking lot in the direction of Hafnawi's Desert Life Camp.

Adrenaline surged through Axel's veins as the visitor center faded into open desert. The road to the camp was nothing more than a well-worn path in the sand. Signs painted on rocks appeared every few hundred yards, indicating they were driving in the right direction. Axel looked to see if the other jeeps were coming after them. No one was on their trail.

They had been driving for a good fifty minutes when Charu began to slow down.

"What's wrong?" Axel asked.

"We're getting low on petrol," Charu said. "I need to save it."

"I hope we have enough to get us there."

"You and me both. The last signpost said the camp is in three kilometers."

"That's less than two miles. We could walk that if necessary."

Just then, a powerful gust of wind blasted the jeep. Thunder cracked over their heads, and lightning bolts sliced through the clouds. Grit and dirt blew in their eyes. The jeep rocked sideways, teetering on two wheels. Charu tried to correct the wheel but lost control. The jeep flipped, somersaulting its way across the sand like a hunk of space-age sagebrush.

The jeep finally came to a stop in a mound of soft sand. Both of them sat there for a stunned moment. They slowly moved limbs and rolled necks, checking to see if any bones were broken.

"Are you okay?" Charu asked.

"I guess," Axel said. "How about you?"

"Nothing's broken, but I feel a whopper of a head-ache coming on."

Charu crawled out of the jeep. A second later, she shrieked at the top of her lungs.

"Wow!" Charu cried. "Axel, this is amazing! You have to see this!"

Axel wiggled free from the wreckage and looked into the atmosphere. What he saw nearly brought tears to his eyes. The once clear blue sky was now the color of an exploded crayon box, a never-ending ribbon of a leprechaun's rainbow.

Chapter Thirty-One
MEGAN

The jet skidded to a stop, mere feet before crashing into the control tower. Miraculously, the pilot had managed to correct the plane in midair and land on the runway. Some passengers wept. Others prayed. Megan let out a long sigh of relief. She held Jag's arm with one hand and wiped off her mouth with the other.

"I'm sorry I got sick," she said.

"Don't apologize," Jag said, taking in deep, slow breaths. "I almost threw up myself."

Megan was still in shock from both the airplane flight and the revelation about her mother.

"My mother's a doomsday cult leader," she whispered, still not quite believing what she had read. "She left me and my dad when I was little to worship the end of the world. I wonder if schizophrenia runs in families."

The sound of sirens blared from outside. Megan stuffed the magazine with the article about her mother in her carry-on. She looked out the window and saw several emergency vehicles racing down the runway in their direction. An hour later, everyone was off the plane with only a handful of minor injuries.

"This would be so much easier with a GeoPort," Megan said to herself.

"What next?" Jag asked.

"We rent a car and head for 29.5347° N, 35.4079° E. That's where we'll find Axel, Charu, and hopefully Daisha. I've done my research on the location. It's extremely remote. Very near several desert tourist camps and not far from the Wadi Rum Visitor Center."

As they stood in line for a car rental, a large crowd gathered around a television monitor. A show reported about temperatures reaching as high as one hundred and forty degrees Fahrenheit in several countries near the equator.

"It's happening," Megan said, her voice filled with dread. "Temperatures like this signal the earth's magnetic field is dramatically weakening. Soon those temperatures will reach far into the colder regions of the northern hemisphere."

"We'll find Axel," Jag said. "We'll fix this."

"Good morning," said the clerk behind the car rental counter. "Would you like to rent a compact, economy, midsize, or full-size? We also have several standard SUVs for rent."

"Standard SUV," Jag said. "We may need four-wheel drive."

The clerk typed into her computer. "May I see your credit card, please?"

Megan handed over the Hatch, LLC card, and the clerk swiped it into a slot. A rejection beep rang out. The clerked swiped the card several more times.

"I'm sorry," the clerk said. "This card isn't working. Do you have another one?"

"No," Megan replied with a sigh. She turned to Jag. "Looks like the Doctor caught on to us."

"Where can we get a bus?" Jag asked.

"All buses and taxis depart from Airport Street outside Gate C," the clerk instructed.

They pooled their cash and purchased two tickets to the Wadi Rum Visitor Center at ten dollars one way. That left them with another fifty bucks for food, bribe money, or whatever. The ride was bumpy and long. They drove through beautiful expanses of desert, but Megan had much more important things on her mind than scenery.

"Do you remember when Daisha went into the X-Point at the Sun Temple?" Megan asked.

"Of course," Jag said. "How could I forget it?"

"The only thing I can think of is that it has to happen again. Only this time with Axel and in the opposite way."

"Daisha accomplished her mission, but we don't even know what happened to her. She could be dead for all we know. What happens to Axel if he goes through?"

A tear rolled down Megan's cheek. Axel's father and Daisha's mother would have known what to do. In fact, if they had lived, none of this would have happened. Megan suddenly felt the weight of responsibility on her shoulders—to protect Axel and Daisha, to safeguard their parents' work, and to save the world.

"I don't know what's going to happen to him," she said, rubbing her eyes. "But we both know what's going to happen to the earth if he doesn't create a new X-Point."

Jag let out a deep sigh. "Say we only find Axel, or just Daisha," he said. "Will one GeoPort do the trick?"

"Common sense says yes, but your guess is as good as mine at this point. All I know now is we have to try something before it's too late."

Megan's mind drifted back to when Larraj had read

her own palm leaf before he disappeared from the caves. The Nadi reader revealed her life like an exposé in a tabloid magazine. He even knew about her mother abandoning the family when she was only four years old. His words still sent shivers up her spine.

You helped the boy with hair like a muddy river die yet still live. Now, it's your turn to do the same. For humans, death is not the end. It's just the beginning. The Earth, on the other hand, only has one life, and there are no beginnings but this one.

The bus rolled down a dirt road and into a large parking lot.

"Wadi Rum Visitor Center," the driver announced. "You can get information on camps, excursions, and activities."

Megan had a recent picture of Axel on her phone. She and Jag walked around the complex, asking employees and tourists if they had seen the boy. No one recognized him. Just as they were about to give up, a man wearing a camouflaged outfit, red beret, and big black boots opened a door and walked outside.

"We might as well ask him," Megan said. "We've tried everyone else."

Megan and Jag rushed outside before the man slipped out of sight.

"Excuse me," Megan said. "May I ask you a question?"

The man turned around and smiled. "Of course," he said. "How may I be of assistance?"

"We're looking for this boy," Megan said and handed him the phone. "I thought he might have been here."

"Is this a joke?" the man asked accusingly. "Am I on an episode of *Hidden Camera* or something?"

Jag gave him a puzzled look. "No, sir," he said. "We really are looking for this boy. He's a friend who may have gotten lost."

The man let out a hearty laugh. "You are the second person today who was looking for this boy! Yes, I've seen him. He was waiting for a bus to Hafnawi's Desert Life Camp. It's about an hour from here."

"That's exactly where we need to go," Megan said. "How do we get there?"

"On tomorrow's bus," the man said. "Last transport there left thirty minutes ago."

"I have money," Jag said. "I'll pay someone to take us."

The man took off his beret and ran a hand through his salt-and-pepper hair. "I know a boy who runs a jeep tour. If you pay, he'll take you. Someone actually stole one of his jeeps today. Follow me."

"Thank you so much!" Megan said. "We really appreciate this."

They took one step toward the visitor center, and the sky exploded over their heads. Thunder, lightning, and brilliant colors rocked the atmosphere. Blasts of hot, highly charged particles rained down on them like giant sparklers on the Fourth of July.

"We're too late!" Megan cried as Jag dragged her from the bombardment and into the visitor center.

Chapter Thirty-Two
MUNI

Muni assembled all of her followers in the large, open-air dining tent. They had just come back from their camel ride and were hot, tired, and hungry. Since the Antakaale were strict vegans, Tala, Ghazal, and another woman served them a large buffet of hummus, stuffed grape leaves, tabouleh, fresh vegetables, and bread.

They chatted quietly among themselves as they ate. Muni watched them all intently, her soul overflowing with unconditional love for every one of them. Unbeknownst to them, this was to be their last meal, and Muni was glad they were enjoying themselves.

Faraw sat at the end of one of the long tables. She bounced Varya on her lap and fed her cucumbers and bread. The child's smile never ceased to warm Muni's heart. She walked over to the table and picked Varya up.

"How did our precious one enjoy the camel ride?" she asked Faraw.

"She loved it," Faraw answered in her thick Somali accent. "Tell Muni what you thought of the camels, sweetheart."

"Bumpy," Varya said with a giggle and pinched Muni's nose. "Will I see Mommy today?"

Muni kissed the toddler on the cheek. "Mommy's going to be very busy today," she said. "I'd like you to spend much of the day with me. Would you like that?"

Varya nodded and buried her head into Muni's chest.

"Perfect." She handed the child back to Faraw. "I'll see you very soon."

Holding the toddler always made Muni think of her own daughter. The memory of her own little *córka* at the same age made a lump form in her throat. She quickly swallowed the emotion and turned her attention back to her followers. They would need much guidance and love today. Nothing could pull her focus.

She walked to the front of the tent, clapped her hands three times, and spoke.

"Give thanks to the Voices!" she said loudly. "Their words and their love continues forever."

"Their love continues forever," the crowd answered back.

"Verse ninety-three," Muni continued. "The entrance to New Earth is but a brief breath. Do not miss the opening, or the Voices may pass you by."

"Do not miss the opening," her followers repeated, "or the Voices may pass you by."

The sound of a car engine whined behind her. Muni turned around and saw Pavana step out of the SUV and run toward their tent. She was alone. The brown-haired boy of her vision was not with her.

"The Voices dictated our hallowed book to me a long, long time ago," Muni said, focusing back on the crowd. "I was laughed at in the beginning. The more I shared the Voices and *The Way to New Earth,* the more scorn and ridicule rained down upon me."

Verse sixty-nine jumped off the tongues of her flock. "The Voices give comfort and compassion!" they shouted. "Their suffering is your salvation!"

Tears streamed down Muni's cheeks at their devotion. Everything about her life made perfect sense at this very moment. She was meant to be here in this place and time to lead her people to New Earth.

"The time has come, dear ones!" Muni cried out. "Today is the day! What we've so longed for is finally here."

Shocked gasps, gentle whimpers, and curious

whispers echoed through the crowd.

A middle-aged woman named Chetana, who in a previous life had been a chief deputy assistant attorney for Ventura County, California, stood up.

"The Voices will cleanse your tears and lead you to New Earth," Chetana said, reciting verse forty-six. "Are we really leaving today?"

Anticipation mixed with anxiety filled the room. Muni could feel their growing excitement. They were all her daughters, but she had to surrender them to the Voices. This was their command.

Just as Muni opened her mouth to tell them, a hurricane-like wind swept up the desert valley. A powerful gust ripped the tent from its stakes and sent it flying into the air. A collective shriek went up from the Antakaale as the first crack of thunder rumbled in their ears. They cried out even louder as lightning streaked across the sky. But when the heavens turned into a giant kaleidoscope of color and light, everyone screamed at the top of their lungs.

"See the top of that mountain!" Muni hollered and pointed in the distance. "That is where the door to New Earth will open for us. Let's go!"

The crowd erupted into a frenzy of euphoria. People wept, and others fainted. Soon, everyone was walking toward the mountain. Muni rushed to Varya and took her from Faraw. She was going to New Earth with the child in *her* arms.

Pavana ran to her, worry etched on her face. "They're gone," she said.

"Who?" Muni asked.

"Gita, Daisha, and that man, Loosha."

"It doesn't matter now. We're going to New Earth."

"But I couldn't find the boy at the visitor center. We don't have the other Golden Jewel."

"Remember my vision, Pavana." Muni adjusted Varya on her hip and took the GeoPort from her pocket. "Daisha and the brown-haired boy needed two of these to destroy the entranceway to New Earth. There are only two in the world, and I have one of them. My vision was very clear on this."

"So that means if we have one they don't have two. There's nothing they can do to stop us."

Muni smiled. "Exactly. I have several packs of zip ties in my bag in the tent. Fetch them."

"Why?"

"Because when we get to the summit, which is a short hike that should take us no more than an hour, we may have some defectors. The zip ties will assure they can't back out before we enter New Earth."

"No one would abandon you or the Voices. We've come too far."

"The Soul Worms can enter a person at any time, even moments before joining New Earth. Get the zip ties and hurry back."

Pavana nodded and raced back to the tent. Muni turned to her followers and saw a single figure staring at her from across the camp. She recognized him immediately.

A pang of fear shivered up her spine.

"The brown-haired boy," she whispered, and jogged to catch up with the group.

Chapter Thirty-Three
DAISHA

The sky exploded above Daisha's head. Thunder boomed. Lightning cracked like a whip. Orange, blue, emerald, yellow, purple, and every color in between tinged what was once a never-ending expanse of blue. A pulsing, nuclear-green cloud appeared in the upper atmosphere. Raindrops of fire sprinkled down.

"Ouch," Daisha yelped as the boiling rain stung her cheeks and bare arms.

A massive gust of wind knocked her off balance. She tumbled backward. Several tents, chairs, and other items blew past her.

"I'll never find Axel," she lamented and crawled under a rocky outcrop to keep from the fallout.

Far in the distance, she saw Muni and all of her followers trekking into the desert toward the spiraling mountain on the horizon. Luciana and Loosha entered her frame of vision. They trailed far behind the Antakaale, but were running to catch up with them. She thought about what Luciana had said inside the tent. They needed both GeoPorts to make a new X-Point. Muni had one. Axel without a doubt had the other, and he was at the visitor center. How could she get there in this doomsday weather?

The rain cloud that had been pelting her with hot pinpricks dissipated in the sky. The thunder, lightning, and wind were still strong, but she managed to crawl from her cover and fight her way forward. She was hoping to see Fahd and beg him for a ride to the visitor center. No one was around. The camp was like a Wild West ghost town. A pile of sand buried the only truck in sight up to the windows.

"Luciana, Loosha!" Daisha called out, but there was no response.

She hiked in the direction of the road. There was a large boulder with a pointing arrow. The signpost read *Wadi Rum Visitor Center—95 Kilometers*. Maybe another car would pass and she could hitch a ride. Hopping on a camel and galloping all the way there passed through her mind. She glanced around for one, but they too had fled the area.

Several whirling dust devils popped up out of

nowhere. They looked like dirty ghosts twirling and dancing across the desert floor. The spinning sand was coming for her. She ran in the opposite direction. With every step, she sunk deeper into the ground.

"Ahhh!" Daisha wailed as the sand began to swallow her.

The drift had blown over her thighs and was moving toward her waist. She struggled with all her might, but the lower half of her body wouldn't budge. The dust devils grew closer, dropping the visibility to near zero. As they were about to suck her into oblivion, two figures emerged from the wall of dirt. They grabbed her under the arms. With a giant heave, they tugged her out of the quicksand.

"We have you!" a man hollered through the howling wind.

Daisha thought she recognized the voice. She tried to look, but sand had caked her eyes, causing temporary blindness.

A female with a thick Indian accent shouted, "Hurry! We have to find cover!"

The two people steered her toward a small crevice between large, jutting rocks. Together, they crawled on their hands and knees to a small cave. Darkness enveloped them. Daisha hacked and coughed, trying to clear the sand from her lungs. She heard a flicking sound, like someone trying to fire up a lighter. After a moment, the flame ignited and a faint light filled the space.

Axel's face stared back at her.

He handed the lighter to the girl and then collapsed into Daisha's arms. Tears of joy streamed down their faces as they held each other tight. She cupped his face, stared into his eyes, and cried some more. Just being near him made her heart swell.

"What happened to you after the Temple?" Axel asked, still clinging tightly to her.

"I went through the Warp and landed back at Centennial Fountain in Palo Alto," Daisha said.

"How...what...why?"

"I don't know the how, what, or why of anything anymore. Remember Boris?"

"Of course."

"He was waiting for me. When Loosha shot us, we ended up inside one of the Doctor's guesthouses."

Axel's face twisted into a question mark. Daisha quickly told him her story, from the random Warping and natural disasters to the Wadi Rum desert and spitting camels.

"We Warped here too," Axel said.

Charu cleared her throat.

"Daisha, meet Charu," Axel said. "She was one of the dancers back at the Konanavlah Sun Temple. I wouldn't be alive today without her."

Daisha smiled at her and turned back to Axel. "Do you have your GeoPort?"

"Yes." He pulled the unit out of his pocket. "This sucker's primed and ready to roll."

"Thank goodness. Luciana says we need both of the GeoPorts to open up a new X-Point. Muni has mine."

Axel scratched his head. "Who are Luciana and Muni?"

"Members of the cult. They call themselves the Antakaale. They want the world to end so they can go to this place called New Earth. But according to Luciana, only our two GeoPorts can stop this from happening."

"I don't understand," Charu said, speaking up.

Daisha opened her mouth to explain when a loud bang came from outside the cave. There was a scraping sound, like two pieces of sandpaper rubbing together.

A muffled female voice said. "I saw them go in here."

"Who is it?" Axel whispered.

"Muni's coming," Daisha said, panic straining her voice.

"What will she do to us?" Charu asked.

The sound grew louder. Daisha heard another voice.

There were two of them.

"Douse the lighter," she ordered Charu.

The cave went black. They pressed themselves against the back wall, bracing for a fight.

"Hello!" the deep voice of a man called out.

"Axel, Charu? Where are you?"

Charu flicked on the lighter. Two figures stepped into the dim glow.

Daisha's mouth fell open. "Megan, Jag!" she cried. "What are you two doing here?"

Chapter Thirty-Four
MEGAN

Megan wrapped all three of them in her arms. They wept and hugged, thrilled at being together once again. Jag turned on a small penlight. The cave illuminated with light so everyone could see.

"How'd you find us?" Charu asked.

"It's a very long story to be told at a later date," Megan said and turned to Daisha. "Please, tell me you have your GeoPort."

Daisha frowned. "I don't," she said. "Muni took it from me."

Megan's mouth dropped open. "What did you just say?"

"I said Muni took it from me." Daisha repeated. "She's the leader of this crazy cult."

Megan pulled the magazine from her bag, fighting the urge to cry. "Do you mean this Muni?" she asked, holding up the cover with Muni's picture.

"That's her," Daisha said. "Why would that crazy witch be in a magazine?"

"Because she used to be a well-respected geophysicist. Until, according to the article, she became ill with paranoid schizophrenia and started a doomsday cult."

"That's really sad," Charu said.

"She also happens to be my mother," Megan said, her voice heavy with emotion.

"What...how?" Daisha stuttered.

"There's no time for explanations now. We need to get that GeoPort so you two can open up a new X-Point. The world is very near the tipping point. The color you see in the sky is really the solar wind pummeling Earth's magnetic field. Did you feel that stinging rain earlier?"

"Yes," Daisha said. She held out her arms. "Look. It left little burn marks on my skin."

"That was caused by the sun's radiation leaking through holes in the stratosphere," Megan explained. "Once the magnetic poles flip, which will be very soon, the problem's only going to get worse. Without our magnetic safety net, Earth will turn into a wasteland similar to Mars in short order."

"Wow," Daisha remarked. "Luciana said the exact same thing."

"Who's Luciana?" Axel asked.

"She's one of Muni's followers. Well, one of her ex-followers I should say. Her name's Luciana Lopez. She sounds smart, like a real scientist."

Megan turned to Jag. "That's the name of the lost daughter those heartbroken parents talked about in the article."

"Muni and her followers are heading to the tall mountain beyond the camp," Daisha explained. "That's where the door to this so-called *New Earth* will supposedly open. Loosha and Luciana are going there right now to get the other GeoPort. Muni also has Luciana's daughter."

"Then that's where we need to go as well," Jag said, and they all filed out of the cave.

The wind had picked up, and the sky throbbed like an exposed artery. The heat intensified as the ozone layer slowly melted from the barrage of solar radiation. Close to home, two more of the nuclear-green, radioactive clouds appeared along the horizon. Megan hoped they wouldn't blow in their direction. As they fought their way across the sand, Megan went over what had to happen when they finally had the other GeoPort.

"Our first task is to get Daisha's GeoPort from Muni," Megan explained. "When that happens, both of you must use your GeoPorts to channel the solar wind and create a new X-Point."

"How do we do that?" Daisha asked. "We've used our GeoPorts together before, and it's never created a new X-Point."

Axel gulped. "Don't tell me we both need to go to the heart of the sun."

"No, just the opposite," Megan said. "You need to channel the solar wind to exactly your location. If both GeoPorts are activated at the same time, given the magnetic properties of this location, it should be enough to establish a new permanent X-Point."

"So we just need to enter the coordinates of the top of the mountain?" asked Daisha.

"That's right," said Megan. "29.6339° N, 35.4518° E."

"Will the numbers change based on their location?" asked Charu.

"I believe those numbers will work," said Megan.

Axel typed the coordinates into his GeoPort, and Daisha recited them aloud. "Got 'em," she said. "Do you know why my GeoPort suddenly started working? For the longest time I couldn't enter coordinates. It only flashed the numbers you told us back at the Sun Temple."

Megan shrugged. "I can't be one hundred percent sure," she said. "But my educated guess is the solar storm somehow reset the unit. Now, if my calculations are correct, this will pull the solar wind directly toward you and open up a new permanent X-Point. Also, this is very important. You two must push the SW buttons at the same time to generate enough power. Understand?"

Axel and Daisha nodded.

"What happens after that?" Charu asked.

Megan didn't answer because she had no idea what would happen to them after engaging the GeoPorts. The research of Professors Jack and Tandala hadn't gone that far. They could explode, implode, or nothing could happen to them at all. The thought of losing them again made her shudder. She swallowed the thought away and continued toward the mountain.

They reached the trailhead in just under a half hour. A sign poked into the sand read *The Seven Pillars of Wisdom*. Megan looked up the mountainside. Far at the top, she saw dozens of people making the final ascent. The two radiation-poisoned clouds were almost directly over their heads. At any moment, the throbbing green clouds could open up and sizzle them all.

"Let's go!" Daisha ordered. "They've almost made it to the top."

They hiked fast up the dirt trail, dodging rocks and loose gravel. A light mist from the hazardous clouds began to fall. The drops felt like tiny beestings to the skin. They shielded themselves as best they could and continued up the route.

The sound of loud groans captured Megan's attention.

"Do you hear that?" she said.

"Yes," Daisha said. "It's coming from behind these rocks."

Daisha peeked around the rocks and shouted, "Oh my gosh! It's Loosha."

Megan rushed over and saw a beaten man lying in the dirt. His face was bloody, and he had a gash on the right side of his head. He was hogtied with zip ties.

"Help me," Loosha muttered.

Jag quickly grabbed a sharp stone and cut away the zip ties.

"What happened to you?" Axel asked.

"Those...women," Loosha said. "At least ten of them jumped me and Luciana. They beat the crap out of me, tied me up, and took Luciana with them."

"Did she go willingly?" Daisha asked.

"No. She screamed and fought, but they overtook her too."

"What should we do with him?" Megan wondered. "We can't just leave him here."

"I'll stay with him," Charu said. "You all go ahead. There's some cover under this overhang."

The group scrambled as fast as they could up the mountain. The higher they climbed, the more the sky turned fireball red. The view reminded Megan of the sun's surface from images taken by NASA. She saw sunspots, solar flares, and solar prominences exploding in the outer atmosphere.

The top of the mountain was just feet away. Loud chants mixed with the booms of thunder like a haunted opera.

"We are not of this earth and neither are you!" a chorus of voices rang out. "Destroy Old Earth and save mankind from the evil of itself! A New Earth awaits all who believe!"

Finally, Megan reached the top. She peaked over the rim of rock. Dozens of women and children stood barefoot around an older woman with long gray hair. An audible gasp escaped from her lips. For the first time in over twenty years, she was looking at her mother.

All of the women wore matching white robes and had tattoos on their foreheads. Most disturbing of all was that their ankles and wrists were zip-tied together, just like Loosha's were.

"That's my mother," Megan whispered to Jag. "The only one not bound with zip ties."

"And there's Luciana," Daisha said. "She's the one on her hands and knees next to Muni. That terrible woman is holding her like a dog."

They watched as Muni reached into her pocket, pulled out a small device, and showed her followers.

"It's Daisha's GeoPort!" Axel blurted. "Let's go! It's now or never!"

"Get the GeoPort at all costs," Megan reiterated, and all four them leaped from their hiding place and rushed the crowd.

Chapter Thirty-Five
MUNI

When the last of the Antakaale's wrists and ankles were bound, Muni walked among them. She looked deeply into each one of their eyes. Their devotion to her was strong, loyal, and unwavering. Even when she made them write their families good-bye forever letters, they did not question her. When they toiled all day in the tea fields of their Sri Lankan estate, no one ever complained of their condition. When Muni locked them in the bunker for days because they had tucked a lotus flower behind the wrong ear, they did not seek revenge. Muni was the earthly conduit for the Voices, and she had all the power.

"I love you dearly," Muni said to her flock. "But the Voices love you more. Their love is forever and unchanging."

"Forever and unchanging," they recited automatically.

"Are you ready for New Earth?"

Ecstatic, joyful cries came from her followers. Random verses from *The Way to New Earth* spewed from their mouths.

"The Voices will grant a New Earth for all those who hear."

"All praise and reverence are reserved for the Voices."

"There are no other Voices but that of them."

"Give your pain to the Voices."

The sky above burned with fury. Intense heat swirled in the air. Hot dust burned their lungs. Still, her followers did not so much as flinch. Even when the biting rain pocked their exposed skin, giving rise to boils and sores.

Muni welcomed the pain. She lifted her face to the sky and allowed the evil of this earth to scorch her skin one final time. Faraw handed her Varya. She draped a blanket over the toddler's head to protect her from the infected hail.

"You and I will be first to enter New Earth," Muni whispered into the child's ear.

A sudden blast knocked Muni off balance. She looked into the desert and saw a scattershot of flaming stones enter Earth's atmosphere and explode like nuclear warheads. The Voices in her head temporarily hushed, and the geophysicist part of her brain flickered with life.

"The flipping of Earth's magnetic fields is nearly complete," she said to Pavana. Her assistant was the only person, besides Muni and the children, who were not zip-tied.

"The rotation of Earth's molten core created the magnetic field," Pavana said. "And now its rotation and electrical conductivity is changing right before our eyes."

Verse seventy-two of the teachings flew from Muni's mouth. "The final test will be with fire and heat!" she proclaimed. "The dry Old Earth will give way to a moist New Earth! Do not fear the everlasting inferno for it is only an illusion!"

"Only an illusion!" the crowd answered back.

"This is the heat and fire the Voices spoke of!" Muni screamed. "Bring me Gita!"

Pavana dragged Gita by the arm and tossed her at Muni's feet. Gita squirmed on the ground in her bindings.

"Gita has been lost to the Soul Worms," Muni said. "She will not come to New Earth with us."

Horrified shrieks erupted from the crowd.

"This is not a bad thing, my children," Muni

said, trying to calm them down. "Let me hear verse eighty-four."

"The lost must lie down so the found may pass over," they answered.

"Gita is the one who is lost. It is foretold in the verses. Before we enter New Earth, Gita's life must end here so we may make passage with cleansed spirits."

Muni reached into her pocket, pulled out the GeoPort, and showed her followers.

"This is the *Golden Jewel*," she said. "It wants to silence the beloved Voices, but we will silence *it*."

She raised the Golden Jewel high above her head, ready to pound the unit into the back of Gita's skull. Out of the corner of her eye, she saw two people charging in her direction.

"Daisha!" Muni growled through gritted teeth. "And the brown-haired boy!"

Crackles of highly charged particles danced on the air. Howling wind echoed in their ears. There was a loud sucking sound, and the ozone layer ripped opened like a wound. The sun's radiation seeped through, making the already unbearable temperature even more scorching. Unable to move their arms or feet, the Antakaale collapsed from the severe heat. They gasped for breath, and from the looks on some of their faces, many seemed to question how they had gotten into this situation in the first place.

"Please, untie me," a follower pleaded.

"This isn't right," said another. "I need to get out of here."

"Don't whimper and beg like dogs!" Muni chastised them. "Enter New Earth with dignity, for goodness sake. There will be no more pain! We are leaving this inhuman world for something far greater."

"Give me back my baby!" Gita roared and swung her bound legs, kicking Muni in the shins. Muni lost hold of the Golden Jewel. It fell from her hand and skittered across the desert floor.

Muni turned and saw Daisha and the brown-haired boy rushing toward her. With Varya still in tow, she ran for the Golden Jewel. The boy tripped over a rock and landed face-first, but Daisha was still bearing down on her.

"Leave us, Soul Worm!" Muni screamed at Daisha.

"I want the GeoPort," Daisha hollered back. "Do you want the world to end?"

"That's exactly what I want to happen. The end of Old Earth means the beginning of New Earth. The Voices have promised this."

"The only voices are in your head. You're murdering

these innocent people, not to mention your own daughter!"

Muni shot her a confused look as they both reached for the Golden Jewel. Daisha had it momentarily, but Muni wrestled it from her hand. The mountain quaked and shuddered violently. The ground below their feet split apart, and Daisha, Varya, and Muni fell into a crevice. Varya wailed as they wedged between the walls. The earth shifted again, sending them slightly deeper into the crack.

Muni opened her mouth and laughed, an insane cackle that echoed off the unstable sides. "Welcome to New Earth," she said as she grabbed onto Daisha's arms.

Chapter Thirty-Six

AXEL

Axel watched Daisha and the gray-haired woman, the one named Muni who was perhaps Megan's mother, wrestle for the GeoPort. Muni was holding a little kid with one arm and fighting Daisha with the other. He could tell Daisha was holding back because she didn't want to injure the child.

He scrambled to his feet and started after her, but collapsed after two steps.

"There's barely any oxygen left," he gasped.

The top of the mountain felt like a sauna on steroids. Hot, thick, scorching air burned his lungs with every breath. He looked around for Jag and Megan. Both of them were on their hands and knees, crawling across the dry sand. Their lungs heaved in and out, desperately trying to take in air.

Screams and cries echoed in his ears. The women

writhed on the ground, frantically trying to escape their bonds. A young blond woman no older than eighteen or nineteen called out to him.

"Please," she begged, her voice barely above a whisper. "Cut me loose so I can go to New Earth. I don't want to die without seeing it."

Axel felt sorry for her and the rest of them, but he needed to help Daisha get the other GeoPort or they would *all* die. He stood up and started walking. His head was dizzy, eyes unfocused, heart rate humming.

He heard Daisha yell, "I want the GeoPort!"

Daisha and Muni fought some more, trading swipes until the ground rumbled beneath their feet. There was the deafening sound of dense rock splitting in two as a large fissure snaked its way across the mountaintop. A horrendous smell like a used toilet puffed from the hole. The stench mixed with the scorching air made him want to pass out. His eyes widened in panic as Daisha, Muni, and the child fell inside the crack.

"Daisha!" Axel screamed as the earth swallowed her.

He staggered toward the fracture, lungs huffing. Desperate pleas and cries came from the women. A pounding headache raged in Axel's head as he peered into the hole. All three of them were trapped between the rocks like tightly packed sardines. Muni and Daisha were still fighting for possession of the GeoPort. With Muni still in control of the prize, he watched as Daisha bit her hand. The woman screamed out and loosened her grip. Daisha began peeling the older woman's fingers back.

"I got it!" Daisha squealed. "Axel, help!"

Axel reached down for her. Their fingertips brushed against one another. He was millimeters from taking hold of her hand when a large boulder smacked him hard on the back.

"Ahhh!" Axel moaned.

He turned around and saw a woman with long black hair. She stood over him, wearing a white robe. Unlike the others, she wasn't bound hand and foot.

"The Voices command us to vanquish all enemies of New Earth," the woman growled and pounded him with another stone.

The blow came down hard on Axel's chest. There was a loud crack followed by searing pain through his collarbone. Axel groaned as she jumped on him. Her fists pummeled his head and neck. Just when he thought he couldn't take any more, a large arm came out of nowhere and shoved the woman away.

"Jag," Axel said.

"Breathe," Jag murmured. "Can't...breathe."

Jag crumpled to the ground, all of his energy spent.

Axel flipped onto his belly and reached for Daisha again. Their fingers intertwined, and he started pulling. The pain in his collarbone was excruciating. He gritted his teeth and yanked harder, tugging her up the crevice wall.

She had almost made it to the top when Luciana screamed, "Don't leave Catalina!"

Daisha looked at Axel, her bloodshot eyes rimmed with exhaustion.

"No," Axel said. "I won't be able to save you again."

"I have to," Daisha said and let go of Axel's hand.

Axel watched helplessly as she plummeted back into the hole. Muni was ready for her. They fought viciously as Daisha tried to wrench away the baby. There was another tremor. The fissure widened, and they fell a couple yards deeper.

"Get the baby!" Luciana screamed.

Muni grabbed a sharp stone that had fallen into the crevice. She waved it wildly at them.

"Stop!" Muni demanded. "Or I'll drag this child to New Earth dead or alive."

Luciana let out a horrified wail. "No!"

Muni pressed the tip of the stone into Catalina's neck. Axel heard a shuffle of feet. He glanced over and saw Megan. She was holding a large stone in her arms and looked barely conscious.

"Hello, mother," Megan said, looking down at Muni. "It's me, Megan. Your daughter."

Muni and Megan stared at each other for a long moment, as if they were searching each other's face for some long-lost bond.

"Megan," Muni said, her eyes misty with tears. "I knew we'd meet again. Do you hear the Voices?" She reached out her hand, beckoning Megan to join her in the hole. "Come with me to New Earth, my dear *córka*. You and I will be the first to pass over."

"Yes, I'll come with you," Megan said. "Help me down."

"Don't do it!" Axel protested.

Megan ignored his pleas and crouched at the edge of the hole. Muni quickly set the child aside and reached up to help her daughter. But as soon as the child was out of harm's way, Megan stood back up, a large stone in her hands.

"Good-bye, mother," she said, and with perfect aim, dropped the stone into the hole. The rock cracked off Muni's head with a thud, instantly rendering her unconscious. Daisha snatched the child, grabbed Axel's hand, and scooted back up the wall.

"29.6339° N, 35.4518° E," Megan said. "That's the code for your GeoPorts." She pointed to the sky. "Hurry up, before it's too late!"

Axel and Daisha glanced up and saw a massive, bubbling hot solar flare hurtling directly at them. Flames splintered off the fireball when it hit the atmosphere. To Axel, they looked like torpedoes of destruction destined to annihilate every corner of the earth.

"We have to Warp!" he screamed at Daisha.

Both of them fumbled with their GeoPorts. The fact that Daisha was still holding the baby made it that much harder.

"The solar flares are coming!" Megan shouted. "It has to be now!"

Daisha punched in the first three numbers and stopped. "We can't do this." She looked at Axel.

"We have to," Axel said. "Look around. The world's about to end."

"No," Daisha said. "I think Charu's right. We need the exact coordinates. If the coordinates don't match where we are, it might not work."

She turned to Megan. "Throw Axel your phone. Hurry!"

Megan looked confused for a moment but then understood. She lofted her phone to Axel, who fumbled with it but then opened up the location app.

"What are our exact coordinates?" Daisha asked.

At that moment, a solar flare smashed into the side

of the mountain. People screamed as globs of molten rock sprayed all around them. A fiery meteorite the size of a basketball flew in Axel's direction. He ducked just before the thing completely took his head off, then he turned back to the phone.

"Come on. Come on," he said, shaking the device to try to make it go faster.

"Daisha, Axel!" Megan pleaded. "Please, it's now or never!"

"Got it!" said Axel. "Type these numbers into your GeoPort: 29.6332° N, 35.4512° E."

Daisha erased the coordinates Megan had given them and entered the new ones as Axel read them.

"Are you set?" Daisha asked.

Axel took one last glance between the screens and nodded.

They held their GeoPorts out in front of them. On the count of three, they pressed the SW buttons on their GeoPorts and detonated into the Warp.

Chapter Thirty-Seven

DAISHA

The Warp exploded all around them like a brilliant sunset. Daisha could feel Catalina's presence in her arms. Another warm, loving presence zoomed beside her. It was Axel. Daisha's heart swelled with love. They were together and flying through the Warp once again.

The three of them zipped along at supersonic speed. Explosions of light and colors danced all around them. Just ahead, a massive rush of energy was bearing down on them hard and fast.

"It's the solar wind," Daisha said, holding Catalina closer. "I hope I didn't make the wrong choice."

The sun's massive stream of plasma and charged particles engulfed them. There was a giant *whoosh* like wind hitting a microphone, and they were swept away in its cosmic force. A vision of the universe illuminated as if on the world's largest IMAX screen. Slowly, the picture began to magnify, zeroing in on the Wadi Rum desert like a celestial search on Google Earth.

They saw the Seven Pillars of Wisdom still intact. The blue desert skies had returned, replacing fiery images of the apocalypse. Jag, Loosha, and Charu were busy cutting the bindings off the Antakaale women. Megan was hugging a very distraught-looking Luciana.

Rocks and earth now filled the crevice that had almost killed Daisha and Catalina. Pavana stood there, staring at the ground, a defeated expression on her face. The filled-in fissure was not only Muni's grave, but also the haunted tomb of their New Earth.

New images flickered on the Warp's artery walls. She saw the Galápagos Islands where she and Loosha had run for their lives from the tsunami. The once submerged archipelago had reappeared. Streaks of brilliant colors streaked across the sky as the auroras returned to their rightful places above the northern and southern hemispheres.

Their magic carpet ride continued across all seven continents. The devastating consequences of destroying the permanent X-Point were everywhere—hurricane destruction, earthquakes, volcanic eruptions, sinkholes, wildfires, avalanches, and landslides.

"Our parents couldn't have known this is what would happen," Daisha said. "If they did, I'm sure they would've just let the Doctor have the technology."

Thick dust wafted around the planet like dirty clouds from the impact of several large asteroid strikes. The natural disasters hadn't spared one country on the planet from the destruction, but the people were helping each other. They saw the young pulling the elderly from ruined houses, rescue workers frantically searching for missing family members, firefighters dousing flames, and police keeping the peace.

"Look!" Axel said, as they soared over a very familiar structure in the Indian countryside.

"The Konanavlah Sun Temple," Daisha said. "And it's intact. The Doctor didn't destroy it after all."

An Indian metropolis came into view. Plumes of black smoke hung in the air. Half the city was in ruins, the other half looked like nothing had happened at all.

"It's Bhopal," Axel said. "I recognize the skyscrapers. Charu told me her parents live in one of them. They're still standing!"

Another picture popped up on the Warp's walls. The image wasn't the skyline, but of three men standing on the steps of a building with a sign that read *Bhopal High Court—Madhya Pradesh*. One of the men was an

Indian official. Daisha and Axel instantly recognized the other two.

"It's the Doctor and Pinchole," Daisha said, not quite believing her eyes.

"What's going on?" Axel wondered.

They watched as the Doctor handed the Indian official an envelope filled with wads of cash. Their old nemesis smiled, shook the man's hand, and he and Pinchole walked down the steps toward an awaiting car.

The curtain closed on the Doctor and Pinchole. A bright light appeared in the distance. Daisha recognized it as the same radiance she had experienced from shuttling through the Warp after the Sun Temple explosion. Then everything went dark. Axel, Catalina, and Daisha spiraled downward through a lifeless void.

A rush of hot wind blasted their faces. Catalina whined, tugging at her ears from the intense pressure. Fuzzy images below them took shape. An enormous, translucent membrane like a kid's bubble wand came into view. They were about to land. Daisha held tightly to Catalina as a cushion of wind softened their landing and they popped through the layer.

"Are you okay?" Axel asked.

Daisha's eyes snapped open. It was daytime. The sky was bright blue. She was lying on her back with Catalina in her arms. Surprisingly, she didn't feel ill from plunging through the Warp. She sat up and saw they had landed right back on top of the Seven Pillars of Wisdom.

"Axel, Daisha!" Megan called.

"Catalina!" Luciana screeched.

Luciana ran to Daisha and swept Catalina into her arms, tears of joy streaming down her face. "You're safe!" she shouted, kissing her baby's face and head.

Charu, who had been cutting the zip ties off one of Muni's followers, ran to Axel and wrapped him in a huge hug.

"I thought you were dead," she whispered. "And I'd never see you again."

"Are you okay?" Jag asked.

"I'm fine," Axel answered. "In fact, we're all fine thanks to Daisha."

Megan walked over to Daisha. "Let me see the GeoPort," she demanded.

Daisha handed it over.

Megan studied the unit. "29.6332° N, 35.4512° E," she said. "The last number of each coordinate is different from the ones I gave you. How did you know the coordinates didn't match?"

"I...uh," Daisha stuttered, her face growing flush. "It was a feeling. I don't deserve all the credit. What Charu said earlier made a lot of sense."

Megan took Daisha's hands in hers. A huge smile spread across her face. "Well, you almost ran out of time and got us all killed. But it was the right thing to do. There's no telling if it would have worked with the other coordinates."

She turned to Charu. "And it seems like you really do have a knack for physics."

"We may be fine," Daisha said. "But the world isn't safe. We have a lot more work ahead of us."

"Why?" Megan asked.

"The Doctor," she said. "It seems we're not done with that guy just yet. Good thing our side has gotten a lot stronger since last time."

Daisha, Axel, Charu, Jag, Megan, and Loosha trekked back down the mountain, the women of the Antakaale following close behind.

LOOK FOR THE FINAL BOOK IN THE

SECRETS of the X-POINT

SERIES

COMING SOON

GARY UREY is the author of the Super Schnoz series, which *Kirkus Reviews* called in its starred review "a winner, especially for reluctant readers." Gary is a graduate of the American Academy of Dramatic Arts in New York City where he has portrayed everything from a Shakespearean messenger to a mime trapped in a box on the subway. He puts his professional theater training to good use every time he sits down to write stories for kids.